STRANGER ON THE SHORE

STRANGER ON THE SHORE

WILLIAM J. BORAK

WB

Copyright © 2023 by William J. Borak. All rights reserved.

No part of this publication may be reproduced, distributed, or transmitted in any form or by any means, including photocopying, recording, or other electronic or mechanical methods, without the prior written permission of the author, except in the case of brief quotations embodied in critical reviews and certain other noncommercial uses permitted by copyright law.

All characters and events in this book are fictional. Any resemblance to any person, living or dead, is purely coincidental. Some of the places named in this book are actual places; however, they have been fictionalized and never existed as they are portrayed.

Printed in the United States of America

2023.07.21

This book is printed on acid-free paper.

Because of the dynamic nature of the Internet, any web addresses or links contained in this book may have changed since publication and may no longer be valid. The views expressed in this work are solely those of the author and do not necessarily reflect the views of the publisher, and the publisher hereby disclaims any responsibility for them.

William Borak Books

Table of Contents

Tragedy 1
Arielle 7
Fallen Angel 11
The Party 23
Breakfast With Arielle 36
The Hospital Visit 45
Detective Ramos and Jane Doe 62
Detective Ramos and Chris 66
The Date 77
Arielle's Challenge 89
Marisa and Chris 104
Marisa's Past Emerges 117
Abbey has a Big Day 123
The Emergence of Ana 132
Ana Plans Her Revenge 143
The Angel of Death Arrives 155
About the Author 187

The inspirational and motivating forces for me writing this story are, first and foremost, my lovely wife Helen, our two fabulous sons Gregory and Michael and our amazing grandchildren Juliette, Hayley and Matteo.

Tragedy

IT WAS TWILIGHT on the beach at the Jersey shore, his favorite time of day. Another summer was winding down, and he was staring out from his deck at the shoreline as the Sandpipers danced on the water's edge in the misty haze of the ocean spray. Chris was ruminating again about an event he had spent the greater part of this last year . . . thinking about . . . Theresa . . . the love of his life. It is, in fact, the one-year anniversary of that event.

He vividly remembers the hysterical call he received from Theresa's roommate, "Chris, there has been a terrible accident, and Theresa's been taken in an ambulance to the hospital. She's been hurt, it's bad, Chris. There was a lot of blood."

Chris was stunned, trying to collect his thoughts quickly. "What happened?"

"What I got from the police is that some young guy ran a stop sign and broadsided her on the driver's side. I don't think she even knew what hit her or if she was ever conscious. I was returning from shopping, and I saw all those police cars and an ambulance and, like everyone else in the area, wandered over to see what had happened. As I got closer and could push my way through the small crowd that gathered, I got this horrible faint feeling as I could make out the one car and that it was Theresa's Camry.

"I managed to flag a police officer and told him I think I knew the driver of the one vehicle. He quickly brought me over closer to her vehicle, so I could positively identify the car, and I saw her plates and the Villanova sticker she had on her back window. He brought me over to these more senior police officers who started asking me all these questions about where she lived, close relatives, and so on. Then they started asking me about my relationship with her and if she had any drinking or drug problems. Can you imagine? I just blurted out, 'Are you fucking kidding me?' I just found out that my best friend was in this horrific accident, and they are asking these types of questions. I just kept asking where they have taken her. They took down my information, and I am calling you from my brother's car as he is driving me to the hospital."

"Did they say anything about her condition?" Chris's only response at this time as he is trying to absorb all that he has just heard. The weakness in his legs grows with every word, and they are about to buckle under the weight of this tragic news.

"No, they wouldn't tell me shit, only kept pressing me for information about her. When they did ask if I knew where she was going, I told them she was probably on her way to see you, her fiancée. She told me earlier in the day, before I left, that you guys had plans for the evening and that she would be leaving around 6:00 pm.

"Chris, it's like once I walked over to the scene, I stepped into some kind of surreal world, and I can't stop crying and keep telling myself she is Okay, maybe she is just knocked unconscious and has some bad breaks and or bruises, I just don't know what to think, I just want to get to the hospital. I will see you there."

With that she clicked off, and Chris entered that same surreal world that Jenny just described to him, and just kept thinking, 'This can't be happening . . . this sort of thing happens to other people, not my Theresa.' Quickly grabbing his car keys off the counter and flying down the stairs, Chris speeds off in his car to the hospital.

Roughly two months from their planned wedding date, Chris has a myriad of thoughts flooding through his brain as he tries to maintain a semblance of speed without driving like a madman on the Parkway. 'Should I notify her parents now, or do they already know?' He hits their contact number, no answer. 'Do I leave a message? No, best wait until I get to the hospital, so I know more and hopefully, they are on their way there as well, coming down from north Jersey.' Chris, who only a few months ago turned thirty-six, and Theresa, in her early thirties, had only dated heavily for about a year and some months, but they both knew they were right for one another and had spent the last few months making all these wedding plans. Chris had already experienced some close personal losses, his mother passed away in his teens from cancer, and he lost one of his former best friends to the war in Iraq a few years ago, but this was his future. They had made all these plans, and everyone always commented on how well they just seemed to complete one another.

Arriving at the Hospital and passing rapidly through all the typical administrative and nursing stations, Chris found Theresa's floor, whereupon he could see Jenny and Theresa's father weeping uncontrollably; she was gone. Just like that, in a whiff of time, a life lost, and countless individual futures radically changed forever. He rushed into the room, and she looked so peaceful, some facial bruises still showing despite the best efforts of the medical staff to address them cosmetically. 'This is just some kind of bad dream. She can't be gone. She is part of me.' Then, as the tears streamed down his face, something started happening. Was he getting lightheaded? No, it was something else; he could feel a presence, a strange soft wafting warmth. He could feel her; she was in the room. Struggling with so many emotions, trembling, reeling, he started to mouth, "Theresa . . . I am here . . . please wake up . . . be here . . . I need you. I love you so much . . . please, please don't leave like this . . . come back."

Suddenly, he hears what sounds like a soft breezy whisper . . . her voice . . . so calm, peaceful . . . "I am here . . . I will always be by your side . . ." and it drifts off just as her father and Jenny entered the room and quickly embraced Chris, mumbling their words of comfort to one another and again, just like that . . . she was gone . . . gone now . . . forever.

Chris, a former successful Wall Street Analyst working now for a Wealth Management firm as one of their Partners, had enjoyed, for the most part, a very successful and highly rewarding financial career, which is why the timing of this tragedy was even more devastating. His relationship with Theresa was reaching its pinnacle at a perfect time in his career. All the dreams of their sharing a fabulous future, and down the road, a beautiful family that they both often discussed, now was just a fantasy. None of this was easy for him to accept. A strapping, six-footer, in great shape, physically and mentally ready to reap all the benefits of a loving relationship that he would be sharing with this incredible woman who had so much to offer on so many levels, now will just be an indelible memory. All his dearest friends, the small circle of relatives and his sister's loving and continuous attempts to reach him were pointless. Chris was raised Catholic, but like so many in his age group, lapsed into just attending church for special occasions, weddings, funerals, and some holidays, but now that wine in the chalice had turned back to vinegar for him. He felt betrayed by the heavens he used to revere and turned into a dour, moody young man given too often to drink, self-pity, and downright despair for someone so young.

"Why her, why now, so young, no reason, is this God's will, his plan? All that spiritual shit can go to hell." He spurned all attempts to get him back to his even-tempered, happy-go-lucky self, an attitude he always used to exude. His personal and work life slowly crumbled before him as much as friends and family tried to intervene. He was a lost soul . . . his lust for life and thoughts of hope and future were just words with no meaning for him. He could care less about himself and others; nothing interested him, and he was no longer the same caring, passionate guy. Someone or something needed to shake his world and rescue his slow downward spiral into despair. His life's journey had taken a turn like a ship adrift at sea, but ever so slowly sinking into an inferno-like abyss, abetted by the heavy drinking benders from which he would often have to be rescued by his closest friends. The emotional component of his heart had been drained, and with his loss of sensitivity, he turned to the dark side, often brooding for days, and becoming downright surly at times to his closest friends and family that attempted to reach out as they sought to help him.

Chris only found solace in the fire and ice of his liquid refreshments as the demons of alcoholism hovered above. In Chris's mind, his life was on the precipice of reaching a zenith point with their impending wedding, when as is often the case in life, for no rational reason, it delivers a series of body blows or slams a gut punch that literally brings the affected individual to their knees. However, the cycle of life continues. Spring slowly emerges from the harsh cold dark wintry days, and with it that ray of hope, enhanced by nature's emerging new green landscape, bursting with flora and warm sunlit days. Everywhere around you, people from all walks of life express their growing sense of optimism for new prospects and opportunities to discover new places, new people and most importantly, the possibility for a chosen few to start their life anew, as Chris would soon discover.

Arielle

BACK AT THE beach, as twilight presented a sea haze that often rolls off the water at this time of year, he could hear a dog barking in the distance but drawing closer. Chris peers to his right down the beach, and through the haze, he sees a golden-brown dog racing on the brink of the shore chasing seagulls. Suddenly, what appears to be a German Shepherd turns somewhat dramatically and heads in Chris's direction. As the dog draws near, he can also see in the distance a young woman jogging in the wake of the dog's trail, shouting, "Abbey, Abbey." And with that, the dog slows down and literally drops a few feet in front of Chris. Panting and staring at Chris, the German Shepherd is one beautiful specimen, the sea water glistening off her beautiful coat.

With that, the young woman also approaches. "I assume this beautiful creature is yours?" Chris blurts out.

"Yep, she is a handful, still a baby, full of life, and clearly a work in progress."

The young woman, late twenties, thirtyish, almost stuns Chris with her enthralling presence. Thick dirty blonde hair, pure honey-like skin, sparkling cobalt blue eyes, roughly 5'8", and from what he can gather under her beachy sweats, a somewhat athletic build. "So, has Abbey mistaken me for a big sitting sea gull or does she smell some treats? That was a rather quick turn from the shore."

"She is a trained Service dog, you know, helps people with disabilities, that sort of thing, but you appear to be perfectly healthy, so not sure why she found you so curious to suddenly turn and rest at your feet. Unless I am mistaken, and you have some sort of disability? I certainly hope not and excuse me for even being that presumptuous."

"No, nothing like that, but how is she on fixing broken hearts?" Chris responds somewhat mockingly.

"Ah, see, she does have the gift to help those in need. She really is a very special canine and, even for her age, has incredible instincts. I hope it is nothing irreversible if you don't mind my prying?"

Chris, in his mind, quickly realizes the leak in his brooding state and seeks to change the subject . . . "Hey, what's your name before I start baring my soul to a total stranger, and where are you from?"

"Sorry about that. My name is Arielle, and my friends and I are staying roughly about a quarter of a mile down the beach from here. I think it's the Anderson's house."

"Well, it is very nice meeting you, Arielle and Abbey, but I was just about to head back to my house and make some dinner plans." Chris retorts somewhat briskly.

"Oh, I hope we didn't offend you in any way, remember service to those in need is our specialty,"

Chris relents and realizes he might have overreacted somewhat. "No, that's cool. You just caught me at a bad time, lost in some sullen memories." As Chris has shaken off his brooding temperament with the whole abruptness of her appearance, he is now even more taken with Arielle's beauty, which is almost flawless and mesmerizing, as he studies her whole persona without being so obvious about it. Simultaneously, her presence has somehow lifted his gloomy demeanor and has awakened a feeling of inner peace and harmony, which he has not been capable of feeling for a very long time.

"We should be heading back, anyway. I need to get back and meet my girlfriends to go shopping. There's this big semi-formal party tomorrow night."

"Really?" Chris responds. "It wouldn't be at the Garvey house, would it?"

"Why yes, I think that is the name I heard. I really don't know them, but one of the girls I am staying with is a close friend. "

"Over on the bay side," Chris retorts.

"Yes, I think so because I was told we need to drive there," said Arielle.

"Well, it looks like we will be seeing one another again, as I am good friends with the Garvey's," Chris replies.

"I would really like that," says Arielle. "I would like to see how you clean up." (Chris, unshaven for a few days, hair all wind-blown and just resting like a tossed salad on his head, in a pair of paint-stained shorts and an old worn T-shirt.)

"Well, right back at you; maybe we will pleasantly surprise one another."

"Hey, the night could be full of surprises. Oh, and so you don't get confused. Most of my close friends or associates call me Ari or just El," Arielle responds as she turns to leave with Abbey at her side.

Chris, thinking of a response, holds his thought and just watches as Arielle and Abbey fade slowly into the thickening sea mist that continues to roll on shore. For the first time in a long time, Chris is truly struck by the natural beauty of his newfound friend and is cautiously excited about the prospect of seeing her again soon.

Fallen Angel

FIVE MONTHS EARLIER, that spring, on an early April morning of 2017, on the Brooklyn side of the East River, lies the body of a striking woman . . . seemingly lifeless, drowned, a suicide, foul play, or some unfortunate accident, a thirtyish, Latina beauty. Two adolescent boys, walking the shore looking for an ideal fishing spot, hear the barking of a dog. Curious, as they want to check out the dog and what she is yelping about, they draw near the dog's location and, with that, make the discovery of the woman washed ashore.

"Holy shit, is that a body?" one boy blurts out. The other older boy quickly moves closer and bends over the body for a closer examination. "Is she . . . is she . . ." the younger teen continues. With that, the older of the two reaches down to try and see if there is any sign of life.

"I don't know, can't tell, and I don't want to start touching or moving her around, could cause more damage if she isn't dead.

This is just too freaky, man. I'm calling 911 . . . hey, we may get on the news or something," he excitedly remarks, but at the same time, he is trying to appear cool to his friend but is absolutely shaken by this incredible discovery.

Once the two boys stake the woman's body out, the dog slowly starts to drift away and heads up to the roadway above the shore. Standing off in the distance is this figure of a person, looks like a woman, hard to tell, with the morning glare of sunlight blinding the boys' eyes. The older boy catches a glimpse of the figure above and calls out, "Hey, can you come down here and help us? We found someone who seems to be hurt really bad."

However, the figure above just calls to her dog and slowly leaves the scene. The older boy shouts out to her again to call the police as well, but no response from the figure. The younger teen sees the figure leaving as well and muses, "I guess she doesn't want to get involved." Then, wondering out loud, "Was that her dog?"

Detective Frank (anglicized for Francisco) Ramos, a seasoned, early fifties professional, mother Caucasian, father Latino, from the homicide division along with his newly minted much younger companion detective, Tommy Haggerty, as well as a host of regular police officers cloak the scene and upon close examination of the woman's body quickly realizes she is still alive and calls immediately for an EMT team. They attempt some immediate CPR to try and resuscitate the unconscious woman; however, she remains unresponsive to any of their attempts to revive her. At the same time, they don't want to disturb the potential crime scene, as they need to have a team from the department's CIS group investigate to see if this is, in fact, a crime scene or just some bizarre incident with no criminal intent involved.

Talking to Haggerty, "Ah shit, was there a struggle, but the ebbing waterline could have washed away any evidence that may have been useful?"

One of the senior officers approaches the detective. "Nothing obvious, Frank. There may have been something of a fight, there is some bruising. The ground just seems to have some of the footprints of the two kids that found her, and they know about as much as us right now."

The detective bellows, "Keep searching the perimeter for any signs of identification . . . a purse, broken jewelry, cell phone, anything, because her body has been stripped clean of any means of identification."

The detective saunters over to the two boys, where detective Haggerty has just taken down all their personal information and statements. Detective Ramos quickly breezes through the detective's notes and, shaking his head at the lack of information, suddenly pauses. "Hey, what's this stuff about a barking dog? Any indication that this dog was hers?"

"No," both boys nervously responded.

"How can you be so sure?"

"Well, almost as soon as we arrived, the dog started back up the hill towards the highway, where it looked like some lady was calling because it appeared the dog belonged to her."

"What did this dog look like?"

"Brownish German Shepherd but moved fast once the owner called out to her."

"And what did this Lady look like?"

"Really couldn't make her out. There was a glare from the sun."

"Was she old, young, short, tall? What was she wearing? Anything at all unusual? Do you think she was here before you?"

"Sorry, officer, but we were so focused on the lady lying on the ground, really couldn't say."

'Fucking great,' Detective Ramos, thinking to himself, 'might have been a potential witness to any part of this, and we have no clue about this mystery woman. Or was she just another New Yorker wanting no part of a possible tragedy?' Okay boys, we may be following up with you, but best you go on your way now." With that, the EMT team arrived and immediately started working on the immobile woman.

Carefully striding along the rocky and muddy shoreline while his eyes continually scour for any clues near the location of where the body had been lying, Detective Ramos now questions the EMT medics and the CIS team. "First impressions?" he asks.

"Right now, looks like she took a nasty fall, and the most obvious damage is to her head, which had been resting by a jagged rock. It was blood-stained and seems to be the primary injury source at this point, which explains her unconscious state."

"Any evidence she swallowed any water, or just washed up here, or was in a lover's quarrel and someone slammed her against the rocks . . . anything I can work with here?"

"Sorry, Detective, we have to get her to Emergency asap." They brace her neck and head on the gurney and carry her ever so carefully as they head up the hill to the highway and the emergency vehicle.

"Alright, let me work a little more with the CIS team, and I will see you at Lennox Hill once I wrap up some things here." As the CIS team was searching all the surrounding area as well as packaging the rock upon which her head was injured for evidentiary purposes and further investigation, there was just not much else to be discovered at this point.

Frustrated, he was hopeful that the mysterious victim would eventually recover so he could put this whole incident to bed quickly and hopefully, there was no foul play involved, but he couldn't help but also think of some worst-case scenarios.

"Hey, Haggerty, what's your take so far?"

He responds, "If I'm catching your vibe, Frank, lots of scenarios for this one. Could have been a crime of passion, jealous boyfriend, or worse, was she a drug mule, or involved with one of the drug gangs that seem so prevalent in that part of the city."

Frank responds as he looks across the river at the majestic NYC skyline. "Yeah, in this city, lots of possibilities and lots of questions. Let's hope for once there is a simple resolution to this one."

They both slowly head up the hill, still surveying the surrounding area for any possible clues with any number of scenarios enveloping their thoughts. Ramos and Haggerty, at first glance, are that "odd coupling" of Detectives as you would find; however, when the captain first paired the two Detectives up, his thinking was that they would complement one another. Frank worked very hard as a young cop, especially given his ethnicity and the racist based comments he had to deal with as he worked his way through the ranks. However, Francisco Ramos was always about achieving Detective level; he was not looking to climb the ranks of any management role; he was always about solving cases. As any of his supervising officers would say, Frank is like a dog with a bone when it comes to solving a case; he just doesn't let go until it is solved or reaches a reasonable resolution. He always had one of the highest clearance percentages at every level, meaning cases were solved. Yes, occasionally he would bend the rules or push the envelope, but never beyond any strict legal limits. Haggerty, on the other hand, was college educated, had a family history of being in the PD and knew all the latest criminal techniques and technologies inside and out; and yeah, he was interested in moving up through the ranks, so he handled the office politics and Ramos the down and dirty aspects of the job.

Walking up that hillside, Frank looks up and sees the streetlights and adjoining cameras that more than likely caught a good shot of the mystery woman that may have witnessed something about this young girl; unfortunately, the angle of any of the cameras didn't capture the shoreline. Ramos called out to one of his fellow officers lumbering up the hill. "Hey, get me the videos from these two cameras." Pointing to the specific areas that he felt would give the best view of the woman and her dog. "And maybe some timing information that could be useful as well."

Ramos heads to the hospital thinking about the possibilities, hoping for the best, along with a host of other cases that he is currently focused on, most especially all this recent gang drug activity, and now this beautiful young Latino woman appearing out of nowhere will be joining the pile of cases on his desk. Haggerty heads back to the police station to work with the officers on getting the videos from the street cameras.

At the hospital, the Detective works his way to a familiar side bar emergency area where the attending physicians of the day work on the most recent victims that arrive for that day. It's almost noon and the hospital, as usual, is a beehive of activity, especially in the ER section. Doctors and nurses take patient input data as well as ordering tests, making preliminary diagnoses when possible or providing emergency treatment depending on the seriousness of the illness or injury. Ramos heads to the designated ER section, where they usually hold any potential criminal victims. Exchanging the usual pleasantries with nurses and doctors he is familiar with, Ramos fires off his usual litany of questions, although somewhat taken back by all the monitors and machines his victim has already been hooked up to. "So, how bad is she? Any other bruises or injuries other than to her head? Preliminary diagnosis? Has she said or muttered anything? Any physical or verbal responses? . . ."

"Detective," the primary attending physician responds, somewhat annoyed and stern. "She suffered a severe blow to her head, and she has some defensive bruises. We are not sure how much blood was lost. Was there much at the scene?"

Ramos was somewhat now taken back, realizing that this young victim's life may be in serious jeopardy, and was not just focused on trying to solve the immediate mystery of her appearance by the river. "No, not really, unless she lost some in the water or it washed away."

"Any evidence of any water in her lungs or signs of bruising? Or that she fought with someone?"

"Well, looks like she put up quite a fight or was otherwise injured by some obstacles, or maybe she even swam away from her attackers. Quite frankly, all attempts to awaken her have failed. With respect to a current diagnosis, she is not just unconscious but has slipped into a coma."

"Just fucking great," Ramos thinks to himself, but feigns some sense of concern for the young lady's current medical crisis to the attending medical staff.

"Do you mind if I just take some notes on her general appearance now that you nice folks have cleaned her up, so I can get some better details on her physical description and send out a report on missing persons in the area?"

The doctor responds. "I would place her early to mid-thirties, obviously dark brunette, brown eyes, olive complexion, about five foot eight, 120 pounds, has an athlete's physique, no cellulite here. Quite frankly an attractive young lady.

"As a matter of fact, if I would have to guess, I would suggest she is from South America . . . Brazil . . . Colombia maybe . . . given her overall physical makeup."

Now Ramos's interest heightens, South American. "Have you checked her stomach contents?" thinking drug mule right off the cuff, especially with all the gang drug activity in the area.

"We can, detective, but take a good look at this young woman's features, manicured hands, feet, and upscale clothes from what we could make out of her garments. This was definitely an uptown gal," responds the doctor. "She either came from money or was a very well-kept woman."

Ramos responds, "Maybe a high-end hooker, escort any evidence of heavy sexual activity or rape?"

"We'll check and do a rape kit and let you know of any other specific findings."

"What about any specific interesting birthmarks, tattoos, or other observations?"

"Well, yes, not sure what to make of this," as he and a nurse slowly lift her body to one side. "Look at these older scars on her back, off the top of my head, looks like old stab wounds or was hit with some kind of sharp object that pierced her skin fairly deep as you can see how it has healed over but doesn't appear to have been medically repaired given the nature of the scarred tissue. She does have some interesting tattoos, a small Eagle with what appears to be a circle of flames with arrows in its talons above her right hip, close to her behind." The doctor raises her bed sheet to show the detective.

"An Eagle with flames and arrows. Any significance, doc?

"Who knows why anyone selects their tats these days? But given she may be from South America; it could be some kind of warrior symbolism or that she belongs to some specific family group or cartel family. Colombia is home to many Eagle and Hawk species. Now look at her other side, there is a beautiful white dove, and that usually is a symbol of love, peace and beauty, so your best bet is to talk with the young lady when she awakens. I have no clue why she would have such conflicting tats."

"Thanks, doc. I appreciate any possible insight into this young lady's past."

"So much for our historical perspective. We need to move her to one of our neurological units so they can do some further testing and confirm our initial prognosis."

"Well, please keep me posted if she shows any signs of recovering, and I'll see if the CIS guys have anything more with respect to her fingerprints, etc. Oh, just to try and confirm with CIS, based on what you can discern from her injury, about what time or how long ago would you say she hit that rock.?"

"I would put it sometime last night, anytime from, say, nightfall to early morning. That's the best I can give you at this point."

"Thanks, doc. l guess that's it for now."

Back at the precinct, Detective Ramos stops at the CIS Unit's lab to see if they have any hits in CODIS or any other sources on the victim's fingerprints. Searching for the lab Director and checking on some other results on one of his other cases, he stops to chat with one of the forensic techs. "Anything unusual on the body of that young homeless person that came in two days ago?"

The tech responds, "Not so much on his body, but plenty in his bloodwork. Unfortunately, lots of oxy and fentanyl."

"Jesus," Ramos responds, "and how old?"

"Best guess until we get any ID, very early twenties." Shaking his head and finding the Director in her office, Ramos asks about his latest victim.

"Sorry, Detective, she is definitely not in the system, and we sent her prints over to the Feds to check on Immigration services and any other related agencies, but nothing yet."

"Yeah, that would make my fucking life too easy to get any good news on this case. I guess she just fell out of the sky. Okay, let me talk with the officers and Haggerty, that worked the scene with me this morning; I have another possible lead I want to check out."

Ramos heads to the Homicide Division and works his way through the halls, and related criminal units, Vice, etc. he pauses at the elevator along with a cadre of other officers, administrative staff, lawyers, etc., reminiscing about the myriad of changes that have taken place at this precinct over the years. How few rows of desks there were, black and white board meetings, the clicking of typewriters, and everything seemed just a little saner back then. Now everyone is in a rush, and everyone is locked in on their computers or checking their cells for texts and emails. However, the most troubling pattern is the overwhelming number of cases that keep rising and their inability to give every case the full attention it deserves.

Arriving at his desk, Ramos asks Haggerty about the videos he wanted him to check out. "Just got the videos for the times you asked about, Frank. If you want, we can take a look right now. I think the video unit is available."

"Let's do it," Ramos responds, as his patience is starting to wear thin.

They stream the video to get to the approximate times the two kids said they found the woman, teamed with the doctor's approximation as to the time she was victimized, as well as the surrounding time before and after, to try and get a fix on the mystery woman with the barking dog. Hope against hope that this mystery woman witnessed something about what may have happened to the victim; otherwise, why else would she send the dog down to her assistance? But then again, why wouldn't the woman herself go down to the victim's aide? All questions Ramos was hoping to get some insight via the camera videos, but nothing. No woman, no dog, nothing before or after the kids discovered the body, nor during the exact time they said they saw the dog, as they did a good thirty minutes before and some twenty minutes after, just in case, for whatever reason the kids got their time all wrong, nothing on the video as Ramos's blood pressure continues to rise.

"Really, can I catch just one fucking break?" He yells at no one in particular. "Let's circulate her photo to all the other local precincts and the surrounding neighborhoods. If necessary, we'll go to the press and TV. Somebody must know something about this woman."

The Party

PRESENT DAY – Labor Day weekend

C HRIS IS PREPARING for his night out at the Garvey's, and for the first time in a long time, he is excited about the prospect of seeing a woman, more specifically, the lovely, enchanting Arielle from the beach. Every year the Garvey's throw a summer-ending beach house party, quite formal for the Jersey shore, as they come from old money. His buddy, Kevin Garvey's father, ventured into the micro-brewery business, as they were already in the liquor industry to begin with and struck new gold, old money spawning new. Kevin, divorced, now very much the playboy, had been a long-time friend of Chris's by chance, meeting at an upscale beach bar one night, both drunk, exchanging tales of old female conquests, screw-ups, and loves lost. The two young men, having much in common from a personal perspective and career-wise, both having made their own financial success on Wall Street, just hit it off and have been fast friends ever since.

As Chris entered the mini estate home of his drinking buddy, he quickly surveyed the existing landscape of people milling about. Many of which he knew from the area and from past parties, and casual friends from his own experience. After having exchanged the usual banter and assortment of dirty jokes with Kevin and his buddies, Chris's focus was on the search for that certain someone. As usual with this specific end-of-summer affair, Kevin always hired a small band of professional waiters/waitresses to bar tend and provide cocktails and assorted Hors d'oeuvres for the clientele. This group of waiters and waitresses were hired out of NYC. They were a group affiliated with a service provided by a charitable organization as Kevin's father was fond of reaching out to various Christian charitable organizations as he was quite philanthropic. As the small band of waiters and waitresses intermingled and served the guests, one striking waitress was in the kitchen fetching the next batch of flayed shrimp and overheard a laugh she immediately recognized. Stepping back for a moment as a stream of memories started to flash through her mind, she knew that voice . . . somewhat shaken, a weakness in her knees. Nervously, she attempted to sneak a peek through the door to confirm her worst suspicion. Surveying the room quickly, trying to home in on the person with that distinctive and familiar laugh, she sees a tall, young, handsome figure, sauntering about in a walk she remembers only too well. "Oh, my God. It's Chris."

Chris, preoccupied with his own search, spies upon a small group of three young ladies with whom he is unfamiliar and, seeing one of his buddies chatting them up, makes his way on over to the group. Using his buddy as a means of introduction, "Why Danny, keeping these beautiful young ladies all to yourself?"

"Ladies, excuse my obnoxious partner, but this is Chris," and he takes it from there.

"So, is everybody enjoying the party, and is Danny spinning his wistful charms or boring you with his stale jokes?"

"No, no, he really is pretty funny," one of the interested ladies replies, and Danny, to his credit, is truly one hell of a comedian and quick-witted, so Chris knows only too well he has loosened this group up quite well by now, but Chris is more interested in addressing his own personal agenda.

"So, let me continue with my little story before I was so rudely interrupted by my so-called friend," Danny continues, while Chris gains some eye contact with one of the ladies, who appears to be a little older and more mature than her two female counterparts.

"Excuse me, but does that empty wine glass need a refill?" Chris asks the lady he has chosen as his target for the evening.

"Sure, and by the way, my name is Sue," as she extends her hand for the customary handshake of introduction.

Chris guessed right; she is the worldly, savvy lady he is seeking in hopes of gathering some intel. Unfortunately, not about her, but with respect to his missing mystery lady. As he returns with her refilled drink, Chris starts his soft inquisition,

"I haven't seen you or your friends around the beach here, or I don't recall any of you from any previous parties, and I am sure I would have remembered you," using his own brand of charm to disarm the young lady of his true motive for speaking with her.

"No, we only recently rented the Anderson home for the last two weeks of August and Sarah, my compatriot over here, knew one of Kevin's work associates, and we were invited. I suspect they were concerned about having a shortage of available women in the area, but I see it appears to be fairly equitable."

The party and music have now picked up in tempo. Chris responds, "Hey, we all have our motives for tempting lovely ladies such as yourself to our annual soiree, and I would say they certainly hit the bullseye with you and your girlfriends."

"Okay, who are you trying to impress?" she responds somewhat warily.

"Okaaaay, laying it on a little too thick, huh?" Chris sheepishly retorts.

"Just a little."

"So, let me back up. Are you from the area, north Jersey?"

"Yeah, Kathy, the shorter one, is my best bud from college, and Sarah and I work for the same firm."

"So, there's just the three of you down here to enjoy the summer's end," Chris says, somewhat inquisitively.

"Oh, so now we are not what you are looking for, boy, do you send some mixed signals." Sue is fairly put off.

Chris quickly responds, trying to regain her confidence, "No, no, it's just that I thought I had met someone who claimed to be vacationing in the Anderson house, and she mentioned that she was coming to this party just the other day, so I guess I am badly mistaken or badly in need of another drink before I make a complete fool of myself."

Clearly puzzled and a little pissed at what Chris's true intentions were and watching him sheepishly retreat for his sorely needed refill, Sue, annoyed but equally dismayed, returns to her girlfriends and Danny's ongoing routine.

Chris pours himself another vodka on the rocks as he is now equally confused, disappointed, and irritated. So, the babe on the beach was playing some kind of game with him or never had any intention of going to the party, but she clearly did mention that she was staying at the Anderson house. Anyway, he proceeded to drown his thoughts, as was his nature these days, in his drink. Steeped in his own gloom, he is abruptly shaken from his minor stupor when a very familiar perfume scent from his past wafts in his direction. He recognizes this scent only too well, but there is a very specific reason he turns to discover the specific source of that perfume because there was one very, very special person that always wore it for all their formal occasions together, and that special person was . . . Theresa. As he quickly raises his eyes to focus on the source of this scent, he catches an exchange between a woman and one of the male guests. Chris's focus rests on one of Kevin's work associates and one of the waitresses. This guy already had too much to drink and was oblivious as to who he was hitting on, but as Chris surveyed the waitress's appearance, he couldn't blame the guy.

Thick raven-colored hair, albeit pulled back for the job, about 5'8", and great figure, although she was in a semi-formal waitress blouse and skirt, but he couldn't help but notice some familiar facial features. Angular face, high cheekbones, beautiful complexion, striking brown berry eyes, and a sly grin that was way too familiar as the waitress waved off her aggressive suitor.

"On the job, no fraternization with the help. Sorry, but that's our policy, and I need this job." Then she went into the kitchen. Again, there was an inexplicable familiarity with her mannerisms and the way in which she dispatched her suitor, a Theresa doppelganger. Chris, all at once, somewhat stunned and bewildered by what he just witnessed, steps back and tries to compose himself and his thoughts. Thinking to himself, 'What the fuck is going on here? How much have I had to drink? Am I having some bad flashbacks and placing Theresa's persona on this unknown waitress, or am I seeing this all clearly? I must check this out.'

Theresa was quite the successful businesswoman in her own right. Confident, beautiful, athletic, smart with an acerbic wit, and could handle any business situation and certainly any male confrontation with ease, all of which is very much why Chris was so taken with her when he first met Theresa, college educated, a tennis star with the college team; was an IT professional who eventually went off on her own with a small group of close work associates and built their own tech start-up company that was doing quite well, with her at its helm just before her passing. Chris was now quietly reminiscing about their first meeting. Roughly two and a half years ago, on a warm early Spring morning, Chris headed down to Chelsea Piers tennis courts with one of his close work buddies. Chris was a decent player but used tennis more as a way to stay in shape and a release from the weekly stress of a hectic work week. In the immediate court to his left were two very attractive women playing an intense game. Without trying to be obvious, Chris couldn't help but notice the gorgeous chestnut-haired beauty with those long-tanned legs breezing across the court like a gazelle. As Chris and his buddy start volleying as a warmup to their game, the ladies in the adjacent court take a break. Now it is the ladies who are checking out the two good-looking young men in the adjacent court.

Chris, picking up on the attention from the ladies chatting and enjoying their water break, couldn't pass the opportunity to open a dialogue with the ladies in between volley shots with his partner. "You gals all tuckered out already? Mark and I pride ourselves on being a very competitive doubles team, but if you ladies are wrapping up or have other plans, no problem."

Both ladies chuckle at Chris's tease and chat about the proposed challenge. Theresa responds, "You really think you two hotshots can take us on?"

"Absolutely," Chris responds, and to further tease the gals, says, "we'll only play our 'B' game."

Laughing at the misogynistic challenge, Theresa says, "I have a better idea. Why don't we make this interesting and raise the stakes?"

Chris and Mark stop playing now and focus their attention on the two attractive ladies. Chris takes the lead again, "how about $100 a game, winner takes all?"

Theresa turns and checks with her partner. "Hey, I thought you guys said you were good? How about $200 a game, winner takes all? Or is that too rich for you fellas?"

"You're on." And with that, Chris invites the ladies to their court.

Smiling to himself, still deep in the thoughts of that day, Chris remembers how Theresa and Tracy destroyed him and Mark on the court that day, but it was after the match, as everyone was toweling off and drinking their assorted athletic beverages, Chris sauntered over to Theresa. Having just let her hair down and shaking her head, Chris was almost stunned by her beauty up close. With her flawless complexion, sparkling emerald eyes, and thick flowing hair just touching her shoulders, he couldn't take his eyes off her. Chris, without hesitation, went in for the charm offensive and eventually won her over. She somewhat reluctantly at first accepts his invitation for dinner later in the week, nothing formal, keeping it all very casual. Chris recalls in his thoughts how anxious he was about their first date and how he couldn't get her gorgeous face and bold personality off his mind. He was smitten big time. Still scrolling down through his thoughts about their relationship and how smoothly and rapidly it all progressed into an all-out love affair; she was the perfect life partner.

So, in what universe is this waitress in any shape or form bearing a resemblance, with respect to personality, presence, and mannerisms, to Theresa, to say nothing of the striking similar physical features? With all of this in mind, Chris enters the kitchen in search of his quarry. Nowhere in sight, Chris asks one of the passing waitresses, "Excuse me. I was looking for a dark-haired, good-looking waitress, about five feet eight."

Before he can finish his brief description, the waitress cuts him off, "Oh, not another horny guest looking to hit on us working girls, look we have a strict no-fraternization policy, and I'm supervising this gig, so take all your charm and good looks back to the party as there are plenty of lovely ladies out there that I am sure would love to make your acquaintance."

"I know this is going to sound trite, but I think I know her from somewhere, and I just want to ask her some questions. You can watch. Trust me, my intentions are quite honorable. She has a striking resemblance to someone who was very important in my life, and I just need a few minutes of her time." Struck by his tone of sincerity and that he appeared to be relatively sober, the supervisor relented.

"Okay, you appear to be genuine, but I will be watching, so please, I don't need any incidents as this is an important engagement for our organization, and we have a reputation to uphold. I think the person you are looking for just went into the lady's room as she is changing her clothes and needs to leave early for personal reasons, so please, no drama tonight, for my sake."

"Thank you, and I promise you no nonsense, and if anything, I will see to it that you and your organization gets a solid recommendation on my behalf as I am a close friend of the host."

"Well then, good luck, my friend," as the supervisor, now feeling more comfortable, goes about her business with a wary eye. With that, the waitress, now in casual clothes, appears, hair down past her shoulders, and minimal make-up, re-enters the kitchen area and stops in her tracks as her eyes pop at the sight of Chris. Quickly, she is the one now trying to gather her composure and thoughts and how she needs to play this impending encounter.

Chris slowly approaches. "Excuse me, let me introduce myself. I'm Chris . . . Chris Reardon, a very good friend of the host of the party, and I hope you don't mind, but I wanted to meet you."

Both Chris and the waitress are trying to take as much of each other in with their eyes while their minds are whirring at warp speed with respect to what they are going to say. "Very nice to meet you, Chris. I'm Marisa, Marisa Flores."

There is that pregnant pause as each one sizes the other up like two prize fighters seeing one another for the first time, but there is a more salient emotion, one that is hanging in the air, a strong mutual attraction that is overwhelming, each one is trying hard to suppress.

"So, was there something I did that offended anyone? I am relatively new at this, as this is only my third time serving at an event like this."

"No, no. Not at all, and this may sound like a line or something, but please, that is not my intent." Chris starts to stammer as he is unnerved by this whole meeting. "It's just I have this unmistakable feeling that we have met before or know some mutual friends or were present at some similar event. Do I seem familiar to you, or do we know one another? My memory may just not be functioning at a hundred percent right now, alcohol and all."

"No, sorry to disappoint, but I am sure I would have remembered if we had met or knew one another."

"I hope you don't mind my being so inquisitive, but do you live in the area . . . or did you grow up around here?"

"Well, we are getting a little personal now, Chris, but no, I live in the city (New York), and I definitely did not grow up in this area."

"Well, I guess I am just having an off night. My bad."

"No problem, but I really have to get going as I have an appointment."

"Yes, certainly, and thanks for entertaining my little inquisition, and I apologize for taking your time." They still are in the trance of observing each other closely without seeming obvious,

Marisa grabs her things and starts heading towards the back door. Chris, not wanting to miss this opportunity to resolve the feeling in the pit of his stomach and pounding heart, "Hey, Marisa, would it be at all appropriate if I were to meet you one day for lunch in the city, as I do a lot of work in the city, so it is no big deal for me."

Marisa, feeling both apprehensive and relieved that Chris made a move to see her again, still plays it cool. "Well, by contract, we're not allowed to socialize with the guests at an event, but if we met by chance in the city, I suppose that would be alright."

Chris, wasting no time, seizes the opening. "Are you free maybe Wednesday? As I do have some business in the city that day, and maybe we could meet in Central Park by the entrance to the Zoo, if you are familiar with that part of the city."

"Sure, that would work, say around 12:30?" she responds.

"Done deal. I know this neat little bistro just outside the park that I think you would enjoy."

"Okay, got to run. See you Wednesday in the Park." Marisa quickly heads to the back door as one of her associates grabs her, and both speaking in fluent Spanish seem to exchange some pleasantries followed by some giggles. As he was heading back to the party, Chris caught just a glimpse of their exchange and Marisa's second language skills. Or was that her native tongue? She clearly carries some Latino features as much as she resembles his beloved Theresa. He heads towards the bar and immediately replays their conversation, her demeanor, her beauty, and the torrent of mixed emotions that are flooding his psyche.

Chris, seeking some solitude as he wants some quiet time to put what has happened into some kind of perspective, finds his buddy Kevin who is now heavily engaged in a touchy-feely conversation with a newfound friend of his own. Chris bids Kevin a quick evening farewell. "Catch you on the beach or over at my place."

"You got it, big fella," Kevin responds. Chris enters his home, pours himself a Bailey's on the rocks, and now shifts his intellectual and analytical skills into overdrive. Thinking aloud, "A waitress, clearly bearing a strong resemblance to Theresa, but obviously has Latino ethnicity, and a proclivity for so many of

Theresa's mannerisms, the way she moves, handles herself with an air of confidence. Seemingly too bright to be just a waitress, well versed in two languages, her voice and accent are nothing like Theresa's, but the cadence of her speech is so familiar. Lives in NYC, not familiar at all with the Jersey shore area, and then there's the most overwhelming sensation that just hangs in the air between us that I know her, and I can't help but feel that she knows me as well." Chris, emotionally and mentally exhausted, drifts off to sleep.

Breakfast With Arielle

SUNDAY MORNING, CHRIS, as is his usual ritual, heads to his favorite little luncheonette for some breakfast with a copy of the Sunday times as he catches up on business news and baseball scores. As he nears his favorite haunt just off Ocean Avenue, he sees a familiar figure sitting at one of the curbside tables. It's Arielle with Abbey comfortably lying by her feet on the sun-splashed concrete. There is an open seat on the other side of Arielle's table, and she is engrossed in reading her magazine. "Missed a good party last night."

"Oh, hey, hi, yeah, sorry about that, but I had a work emergency."

"Really, on a Saturday night?"

With that, a waitress appears with whom he is familiar. "Hi, Chris, the usual or something different this morning."

"Uh, you know what? I'm up for some French toast and ham, the usual OJ and I could use a strong cup of coffee first." He gestures to Arielle, and she waves him off that she is good. "Well, that should do it."

"Okay, I will get that coffee right out, Chris." The waitress heads back inside to the counter area.

"So, what is it you do that requires your presence on a Saturday night?"

"I'm in Communications and Public Relations, and every now and then we have a client crisis, and I get the call."

"Interesting. You must have some high-profile clients that demand that kind of attention."

"Unfortunately, I don't have the luxury of choosing who or when, which is why I am on call 24-7."

"Well, I hope they are making it worth your while financially, and you seemed like such a free spirit when we first met. I would have never figured you for one of those high-pressured jobs."

Their conversation is intermittently interrupted by the waitress serving Chris his coffee and morning meal. "Are you sure I can't get you anything?" Chris asks.

"No, I'm fine, but thanks."

Changing topics, Arielle queries, "So tell me, what did I miss at this party? Did Mr. Chris meet anyone of interest?"

"Well, I was expecting a certain enchanting young lady with whom I thought there was a connection, but as we both know, she never made it." Both softly chuckle at Chris's small dig. "But as a matter of fact, towards the end of the evening, I did meet someone that, let's say, is intriguing at this point."

"See that, I am a firm believer in that everything happens for a reason," replies Arielle ever so slyly. "And if you recall, I did say the night could be full of surprises."

Chris pauses and gives her a sarcastic grin. "Yeah, but I think I had something different in mind, and with that young lady from the beach." Chris continues to gaze into her mesmerizing, sparkling blue eyes.

"Well, I don't know if I should be flattered or insulted that you would think I would be so easily swept off my feet, to say nothing that maybe I might have found greener pastures with somebody else."

Ouch. OK, peace. So, what're the chances of us making a fresh start and we have dinner tonight or some evening this week? I still find that lady from the beach quite fetching." Chris pours on the charm.

"Boy, you are good, but wait a minute, I thought you already found someone . . . intriguing, as you put it. So, what does that make me, second banana?"

Chris quickly realizes he is in for a challenge and slows his advances. "All I am asking is just for a friendly dinner as an opportunity for us to get to know one another. We really know very little about one another. All I know is that I think you are one lovely young lady, and that any guy worth his salt would love to have dinner with."

Arielle, smiling, says, "Tell you what, that is very sweet and thoughtful, but there is one small flaw in your overall thinking of our situation, and that is that you think I am available."

"Really? I guess I did make that assumption just given your inviting and light demeanor, and I always pride myself on reading people. Boy, did I blow this one?"

"Sorry, Chris, but believe it or not, I am in a very involved relationship and quite faithful to him."

"Lucky guy. He must be someone very special."

"That he is," Arielle responds.

"Well, I hope it all works out, but can we at least remain friends?"

"Absolutely. As I told you, Abbey and I are all about helping our friends and those in need. In that regard, we will always be at your service and available, but as I mentioned earlier, duty does call, so I need to take off, as I am already late for my next appointment. As always, Chris, stimulating conversation and delighted to see you in a sunny, rambunctious mood as opposed to when we first met."

Chris reaches for his wallet, which now has fallen out of his pocket; bending down to retrieve it and his newspaper scattered all over the ground, he responds to Arielle's last comment. "Well, yeah, I always enjoy our little encounters . . . What the hell?"

He looks around, and there is literally no sign of Arielle or Abbey. With that, the waitress appears to see if Chris is ready to pay his check. "Hey, did you happen to see in what direction the young lady I was chatting with took off?" queries Chris.

"Sorry, Chris, not sure what you are talking about, but which lady are you referring to?" responds the waitress.

"The beautiful babe that I have been talking with all morning while I was having breakfast," Chris says, somewhat astonished that the waitress seems clueless as to whom he was referring.

"Chris, the only person at this table was you, and I assumed you were talking on your wireless earpiece, as you often do. So, I made a point not to disturb you."

"Wait a second. You're kidding me, right? You didn't see the lady I was talking with over breakfast the whole time you went back and forth serving this table or earlier before I arrived? You're telling me there was no one else at this table?"

"Chris, I don't know if you are pulling one of your jokes or just having a freaky morning or something, but there has been no one else at this table but you, and yes, I saw and heard you talking, but like I said, I just assumed you were talking with someone over your wireless earpiece."

Now Chris is really beside himself, somewhat embarrassed by his accusations to the waitress, as well as annoyed, bewildered and just at a loss for words as he is sitting there. The waitress retreats to the inside of the restaurant, and she senses something is amiss with Chris.

The more he thinks about both of his meetings with Arielle, the more he becomes angry, mystified and just plain frustrated by this whole crazy process. He wonders if he is hallucinating from all the drinking and if she is some kind of alter-ego apparition. Just how fucked up is his head? The more he thinks about the whole situation he can feel his blood pressure rising and the anger growing within him, and all the dark thoughts that have haunted him arise as he feels like he is being played like some kind of fool. Chris rises from the table, seeks his waitress friend, apologizes, trying to make the best of the situation with some goofy remark that he was just teasing her, gives her an extra tip, and quickly retreats to his car.

Chris driving nowhere in particular along the ocean side, suddenly spies a Church up ahead that he had attended numerous times for different special occasions and stops the car. Realizing it is Sunday and that a mass is probably in session, he slowly gets out of his car and makes his way to the Church. Sitting in the back, paying little attention to the ongoing Mass, he just stares around at all the stained-glass windows and religious figurines that adorn the church, which is old but quite distinctive and appealing in its own right. With a myriad of thoughts still racing through his mind, he happens to catch a scene of a group of angels hovering around a Jesus-like figure, and he just stares and stares. Deep in thought and with that image on the stained-glass window, he replays so many of Arielle's words, "service to those in need is our specialty . . . in Communications and Public Relations . . . on call 24/7 . . . quite faithful to him . . . call me El," and the most frightening aspect to the whole thing, the more he delves into the whole replaying of events, no one, no one else has actually seen this person or knows that she exists.

Thunderstruck, his brain reeling from any reality, he struggles mightily to make any sense of what he has just experienced. He keeps telling himself, "Impossible. Why is all of this happening to me? What does it all mean? I need to get my act together." He pauses, and before he makes a move to leave his seat, he slips onto the kneeling bar in the pew and does something he has not done for a long, long time; he starts to pray and ask for help because either he is losing his mind or something very, very bizarre is happening in his life. He completely does not understand and, to some extent, is suspicious of what lies ahead.

Walking back to his car, Chris slowly feels a warm calmness and inner peace, as well as a sense of rejuvenation that he has not experienced in quite some time. It was as if a great weight had been lifted. A new sense of awareness as to the power of prayer and meditation had finally enlightened him to the fact that, yes, returning to the spirituality of the Church that he enjoyed as a much younger man is not such a bad thing and something he needs to embrace and foster as he moves ahead with his life. There was for him as a young boy and man an inner confidence and strength of purpose that prayer and his faith had always seemed to sustain him during any challenge that life would place in his path. With this emerging 'rebirth' of his faith, Chris seemed to gain a new clarity of thinking and peacefulness that is now providing him with that old confidence and mettle to face whatever new challenges may lie ahead. As Chris drove away, still thinking about his latest episode with Arielle, a shrouded figure with her faithful companion at her side stands on the beach head across from the Church. Kneeling, she whispers, "Mission one accomplished; now our assignment truly begins," as she fades into the breezy, misty winds of the sea and shore.

That afternoon Chris, while at home with all these thoughts of his breakfast experience, his Church visit and his overwhelming feeling of self-assurance, shifts gears to his plans for the upcoming week. Work, and yes, I have a date with this very intriguing, beautiful young lady on Wednesday, but given the return of his newfound mental acuity, he starts thinking, 'What do I know about this Marisa?' He googles her full name, Marisa Flores, and a whole range of people pop up on his screen; he transitions to one of his worksite people finder sites that is more specific and enters as much as he knows about her to narrow his search, approximate age, NYC, etc. Finally, he finds the person that best matches his search criteria and gets an address, name, and little else. He checks for prior addresses. Nothing, parents, siblings, more unknowns pop up, work history, unknown. What the hell? Advancing his search, he finds a link related to her name. Up pops a newspaper article about a missing person found on the East River that spring. He reads the details of the article; 'unconscious, in a coma for weeks, no known relatives, etc. Anyone having any information, contact the NYPD 69th precinct on 9720 Foster Ave. Brooklyn, Attn. Missing Persons Bureau—contact Detective Ramos.' He stares at the accompanying lifeless face pictured in the attached article.

Chris finishes reading the article and sits back, thinking, 'What the fuck? Really . . . really? Is this something I want to deal with right now? This chick is . . . maybe that missing person, for Christ's sake? This is fucking unbelievable.' Chris sits thinking, thinking, but there is that undeniable feeling that there is some irresistible connection between the two of them. His thirst for knowing more about her is undeniable, to say nothing of her striking beauty and haunting resemblance to Theresa. Trying to rationalize it, he thinks to himself, 'Well, she clearly was real, so let's forget all this hokey pokey stuff for now. She handled herself professionally, and she seemed quite normal. If anything, she was quite sharp, spoke two languages fluently, and was very personable, and I may be way off base here; if nothing else, I could just swing by the police station and see if there is a connection. I might just be overthinking this whole situation. I need to get back to the office by Wednesday; I'll swing by that police department and see if I can meet with this Detective Ramos and then just take it from there. Given recent events, how much more outlandish can my life get?'

The Hospital Visit

FOUR MONTHS EARLIER – (May 2017)

THE YOUNG LATINA victim that washed up on the shore lies in a coma still at Lenox Hill hospital, hooked up to a variety of monitors. For the past month, there had been no claims as to who knew this beautiful young woman. There were no reports of her missing locally, nationwide or as a potential visitor from a foreign country and, most puzzling of all, no known identity. A frustrated Detective Ramos is standing at her bedside, briefly looking at her charts after checking with the doctors; no news, only that they would be arranging to move her off-site to a city-sponsored Medicaid-supported hospice center because of the ongoing costs. Detective Ramos, who has been stopping by from time to time just in the event there was some change in her condition, reluctantly moved her case from a criminal investigation and referred it to the missing persons bureau, but there are just too many unanswered questions about her case that made it hard for him to let it go. Off he went about his business to the precinct to investigate the most recent batch of never-ending criminal case activity that constantly besiege the city.

That very night, well after visiting hours, stands a hooded figure leaning over the motionless figure lying on the hospital bed. As the attending night nurse swings by, she stops dead in her tracks, stunned by the hooded figure. "Is that a dog sitting beside the foot of the bed?"

The hooded figure gracefully swirls, motions to the sitting canine, and swiftly exits the room. The nurse, temporarily held speechless by catching the vision of the beaming crystal blue eyes of the youthful, hooded figure and by the dog's presence in the room, quickly recovers and calls out to the departing pair, "Wait a minute, are you a relative? Do you know this woman? Stop. We need to speak with you." With that, the neurological and vitals monitor starts to beep rapidly as the mysterious visitors depart through an emergency stairwell door down the spiraling staircase. The nurse, torn between responding to the patient's urgent needs and pursuing the intruders, heads to the main desk to alert security, describing the hooded figure and accompanying dog to be stopped at any of the main exits of the hospital. Concurrently, what had been a normal quiet night with the individual nurses making their rounds has now turned into a somewhat chaotic scene as there is a stat call to the coma patient's side as well as a security alert. A small team of nurses and attending resident doctors rush into the victim's room to check on her fluctuating condition, as detected by medical monitors.

There is an immediate flurry of activity around the victim's bedside. Doctors, nurses, interns, and the night nurse off to the side speaking with the nighttime Security Supervisor. All the medical monitors fluctuate between normal and higher ranges, indicating that there is new brain activity and rapid eye movement behind the closed eyelids of the patient. With the resident neurologist taking the lead, he checks her eye movement and response to other physical stimulant tests on her hands and feet, which for the first time respond ever so slightly. There are gasps all around. Battling the incredibly thick fog and haze enveloping her thoughts and her eyesight, the victim opens her eyes, straining to gain some focus on her surroundings and the people hovering around her. At the same time the doctors remove the tubes in her throat as she has been in a coma for quite some time and a nurse gives her some water to sip in order to moisten her throat. Her voice quivering, struggles to voice in a stumbling whisper, "Donde estoy?" (Where am I?)

As there are brief exclamations of joy and some tears from surrounding staff, the neurologist asks everyone to clear the room, except one of the residents and the night nurse (Rosita), as she speaks Spanish and has been closely attending this patient since she first arrived under their care.

Rosita explains in Spanish that she is in a hospital and has suffered a bad head injury. The patient tears up when Rosita asks, "Como te llamas?" (What's your name?).

"No se." (I don't know). Tears now start to stream down her cheeks. The doctor, observing that the patient is clearly distressed and upset, asks the resident to administer a mild sedative while he continues to focus on his examination and gets ready to dismiss Rosita. But Rosita swiftly queries in a whisper, "Habla Ingles?" (Do you speak English?), to which she responds in a somewhat now startled expression, "Si." (Yes.)

Somewhat shocked but relieved by this new revelation, the neurologist insists that Rosita leave the room for now as he and the resident will need to run some basic tests to ensure the stability of the patient's condition so there is no lapse or unexpected new developments.

Rosita's head is spinning with the incredible sequence of events, and she rushes back down to the main desk on the floor. Rosita had developed something of a relationship with this patient given the comparable ethnic backgrounds, the patient's youth, and the unusual circumstances that there had been no claims for her identity. Rosita, when time permitted on her shift, would often read various passages from the Bible as Rosita was a very religious woman in her early fifties and developed an affection and kinship with the lovely young victim. Rosita meets again with the Security Supervisor to see if they have apprehended the mysterious hooded visitor or if they have seen the accompanying dog. He quickly explained that they were still checking all the exits and had even initiated a search as he called in some additional staff to secure the entire facility, but so far nothing to report. "Okay, please keep me posted should you find anything."

Rosita quickly realized she needed to contact that Detective whom she had met a few times briefly when he would make his unexpected visits. The main desk had his contact information, and she left word at his precinct that she would be available the next morning to speak with him. She had already arranged to extend her shift through that night and well into the next day as she wanted to make sure her special patient would be getting the best possible care during the night should she need a comforting face.

That morning, after getting all the required visits by any number of medical specialists, including the resident psychiatrist, the anxious victim was resting somewhat comfortably. Based on the latest tests, other than acute amnesia and physical weakness from being in a coma for a month, she was in excellent health as her accompanying head wound and related bruises had more than healed by now. Detective Ramos is at the main desk and meets with the appropriate attending physicians to get the full update on her condition and suppressing his own anxiety about meeting with the patient; he first asks to meet with Rosita privately. Rosita enters a small conference room to meet with the Detective, tired but still pumped with adrenalin at the prospect of developing a new relationship with her special patient. The Detective also had the Director of Security in the room as he was going through his report when Rosita arrived.

"Okay, Mr. Humphrey (Director of Security), I see in your report that last night your security team received a call from Nurse Rosita here at 10:15 pm about a hooded figure and a medium-sized dog in Jane Doe's room and then fled down an emergency exit. Following her call, your team immediately secured all the exit areas of the hospital but never captured any sight or evidence of this hooded figure or any dog? Also, your team conducted a search throughout any potential areas that they may hide."

"It's all there in the report, Detective."

"Any chance she could have changed out of that hoody and used it to hide the dog and carry it out under her hooded garment?"

"It's possible, but I seriously doubt it, as that dog was a decent size to hide."

"It also says here you and the night shift checked all the cameras for that time as well as the camera over Jane Doe's room, but your equipment is experiencing some technical difficulties. What's that all about?"

"Uh, it's probably best I just show you, Detective."

"Okay, Okay, why don't you go to your security control room, and I'll meet you there while I talk with this nice nurse who has been kind enough to wait for me."

"Just so you know, Ms. Rosita, this is not the first time I have come across this hooded figure and that damn dog, and their connection to our Miss Jane Doe lying in that room, so you will have to excuse me if I come across a little testy about this whole situation. I want you to walk me very carefully through your entire experience with this woman in a hoodie and that freaking dog, and please, no detail is too insignificant."

"Well, Detective, it was around a little after 10:00 pm as I was conducting my night rounds for the rooms on my shift, when I noticed a bright light emanating from . . . uh . . . Jane Doe's room, as you are referring to her."

"You're sure about that time?"

"Yes, I saw on the TV by the main desk that the 10 o'clock news was just starting, and that is when I conduct my lights-out night rounds."

"Okay, so now, when you approached Jane Doe's room, was the hooded figure holding some kind of light, or what attracted you to the light in that room?"

"Well, not really. All I noticed at first was that there was this hooded figure kind of leaning over the patient, almost as if she were whispering or praying over the patient, but at the same time, I saw this sitting dog leaning with its head on the foot of her bed."

"Let's hold it right there," says Detective Ramos as he feels that uneasy and exasperated feeling again. "First, what about that light . . . was this figure holding a flashlight or any kind of cell phone light? What?"

"Well, I didn't see any visible flashlight or anything. I guess it was just a kind of glow, an incandescence that was emanating from the room."

"Really? A glow?" Now the Detective's blood pressure is starting to rise. "Excuse me, Rosita, it's all right if we get a little personal here. We seem to be close in age, both Latino backgrounds, right?"

"Yes, Detective."

"Call me Frank, or Francisco, if you are more comfortable, but I must ask you . . . any drinking that night? You into some of the local scripts, weed, any problems like that? Because I will check you out if there's any history, but I would keep that just between us."

"Detective," somewhat indignantly, Rosita responds, "absolutely not."

"I just need to be one hundred percent sure that you had a clear head last night because you are the first credible witness to this whole frigging dog person, okay, Rosita? My apologies, but I had to ask. So, this hooded figure, tell me exactly what she was wearing, height, male, female?"

"Oh, she was definitely female, about five foot seven, and it was a light gray, almost soft silver-like flowing garment, almost like a robe but not exactly . . . almost something like a Nun's outfit but with just the hood draped over her head, no headpiece or anything like that."

"Okay, this is good, finally something to work with; keep going; again, don't leave out any detail."

"Well, I think my entrance into the room surprised her, but she turned so quickly to leave and when I saw that dog, I guess I was equally startled."

"Did you get a good look at her face?"

"Well, yes and no. She was youthful, maybe late twenties or early thirties at the most, beautiful complexion from the little that was exposed, but those eyes, the most beautiful color of blue I think I have ever seen, and it was like they were shining."

"Hair color, any other distinguishing marks? What else, what else did you notice?"

"That's really it. Nothing else was really exposed, and she moved so quickly."

"She never spoke?"

"No."

"What about the dog? Didn't she give it any kind of command to leave with her?"

"No, it moved as swiftly as her out the door."

"When she left, didn't you try and stop her?"

"Detective, everything was so strange, her appearance, the dog, those eyes, but then as I shouted at her to stop or if she knew the patient, all the monitors started beeping, so my first instinct was to run to the patient, but with that, she found the emergency exit and took off down the stairs and at that time of night there are really no visitors or anyone else around as we are all just doing our standard lights-out rounds and checking our patients' vitals."

The Detective intently observed Rosita as well as rapidly scribbling down his notes. "Tell me about this dog."

"Oh, that's easy. I know my dogs. A golden-brown German Shepherd about medium size, not that old."

"You are absolutely sure about the dog and no other distinguishing marks or characteristics about that dog?"

"No, not really, other than she really seemed to follow her mistress without question, like they had been together for quite some time."

"This is very good, Rosita, really. Finally, we have some descriptive data to work with and maybe before you start your next shift, it would be great if you could stop down by the precinct and give our sketch artist some of the details you just shared with me and maybe some other details will come to you while you work with them."

"No problem, Francisco." Rosita finally started to relax and smiled ever so slightly as her long night's journey into the day was finally ending.

"Oh, two more things. First, could you walk me through exactly how our hooded friend left Jane Doe's room?"

"Sure, as I was calling out to her to stop or if she knew the patient, she headed directly to that emergency exit."

They both walked over to the door marked 'Emergency exit,' which was about forty feet from Jane Doe's room. As the Detective attempts to open the door, he notices it requires a pass key card, so the door doesn't open.

"You said you saw her just open this door, no bells or beeping, and just head down the stairwell behind here?" Rosita gives the detective her pass key to slide past the lock, and the door opens.

"Did you notice if the hooded lady had anything in her hand, like a pass key to open that door, or did she just turn the handle and the door magically opened?" he asks somewhat sarcastically.

"Now, Detective, it all happened so quickly, and my attention was distracted, but I am almost a hundred percent certain that she just grabbed the door and fled down the stairwell."

"With the dog?"

"Yes, with the dog right at her side."

"How do you explain that?"

"Detective, that's your job. I can only tell you what I saw."

"Okay, let me find out what the cameras tell me." He looks at one of the cameras in the hall pointed directly in the direction of that emergency door.

"The very last thing for now, as you have been most helpful, Rosita. And again, I apologize for my frustration, but you must agree that this is beyond being just a little hinky."

"Detective, I was there, and I'm still not sure I believe all what happened."

"Okay, Okay, let me make sure I fully understand what happened next. After this all went down, the doctors were checking on Jane Doe's condition because all the monitors were going off and . . . now . . . after almost a full month . . . she suddenly awakens within minutes of the visit by our mysterious, enchanting spirit lady and her canine shadow!"

"That's basically accurate, Detective."

"The Doctor said you were the only one who spoke with our Jane Doe. Is that correct?"

"Yes."

"Exactly what were her first words and anything else she might have said?"

"She asked, 'Where am I?' in Spanish. I then explained, in Spanish, that she was in a hospital and had suffered a bad head injury and had been in a coma for several weeks."

"How did she respond? What did she say?"

"She started to weep, and I asked her what her name is, and she responded that she didn't know."

"Without any hesitation or change in demeanor?" the Detective queried.

"Without any hesitation, in fact, she just started weeping more and was becoming upset, and with that, the attending doctor asked me to leave, but I did ask her rather belatedly if she spoke English, and she responded with a yes and I had to leave the room as the intern with the doctor was administering a sedative to quiet her down, and they wanted to focus on keeping her stable."

"That's everything?"

"That's everything," Rosita responded to the detective's final question.

"Rosita, you have really been wonderful. Here's my card. Please make sure you stop at this address for the precinct and ask for me. I will get you with our sketch artist, and I may have a few follow-up questions, and of course, as your head clears or you think of anything else, please, please, give me a call."

"I can go now?"

"Absolutely, but don't forget we got a date with the sketch artist."

"Yes, Detective, yes."

With that, Ramos stares at his notes. Now back at the room with Jane Doe, torn between wanting to start quizzing the source of all his consternation, Jane Doe, and the Security Director, he opts to first head to the Security Control room to review what the cameras may have captured as he sees some doctors working with Jane Doe.

As Detective Ramos enters the Security Control room at the hospital, he calls over to Mr. Humphrey, who is hunched over a set of security screens with one of his tech advisers.

"Please, tell me you got something for me?"

"Well, Detective, I will let you see for yourself, but here's the deal. We first started with what we knew best from Nurse Rosita's timeline as to when this person with the dog left Jane Doe's room, around 10:15 last night. And we checked well before that time and after. Here you can see Nurse Rosita enter the room at 10:17 pm. You see her expression change, and as she starts to turn away and shout at someone. See that flash of light that blurs the rest of the frame out?"

"Wait," Ramos responds, "back this up, and can you give me frame by frame?"

"No problem," Mr. Humphrey instructs his tech assistant to accommodate the detective's request, and they focus on the sequence of the frames. As before, even with the framing sequence, that shadowy but bright flash blocks out only that area where the hooded person and dog would have left right past Nurse Rosita.

"Are you having any issues with any of your cameras?" Detective Ramos queries.

"Not lately, Detective. Here is the present view. You can clearly see Jane Doe's room entrance."

"Did you do a timeline backup to see when the hooded lady might have entered Jane Doe's room?"

"Yes, but you're not going to like what you're going to see. I think we narrowed it down to exactly 10:03 pm as when she might have entered the room but check this out."

They look at the screens intently and again, as the time frame sequence reaches 10:03 pm, there is that same shadowy flash of light blurring the appearance of anyone entering or leaving Jane Doe's room.

"You gotta be fucking kidding me. You're telling me this is when you think she and that fucking dog entered the room, and all we have is a blurred light? There must be something wrong with that camera. What about the emergency door? I saw a different camera pointed right in the direction of that door. Now she had to hit that door right about 10:18 pm if she left Jane Doe's room at 10:17 pm, because it's only a few feet away."

"You got it, Detective; take a look at those screens."

They watch the video sequence from about a minute before and clearly see the closed emergency door, and right at 10:18, the emergency door is partially blurred out by the same flash of light as it opens and closes with no evidence of any specific person opening and closing the door. Detective Ramos slumps back in the chair and starts muttering a stream of curses in Spanish to himself.

"Let me ask you a question. Is it possible she used some kind of hand laser or other technical device to knock those cameras out?"

"Of course, it's possible, but here's the problem, first, she would have to know the exact location of the cameras, and do it while she is on the move, and when you knock out one of our cameras, it blanks out the whole screen for about fifteen seconds before the cameras re-synchronize themselves. We would get a completely different visual on the screen, not what we have been viewing so far."

"Should I ask about a timeline as to when she left or when she may have actually entered the hospital?"

"Actually, it's even a little more bizarre."

"Okay, lay it on me. What the hell?"

"Well, it appears from what we were able to track based on where she left from the emergency stairwell, she most likely exited out the entrance area where all the emergency vehicles come and go, and we have some security people posted at that actual location to make sure only emergency personnel with patients arrive or leave to go on call."

"So, you have actual people at this location, and surely they would have, at a minimum, seen the dog?"

"You would think so but take a look at this video on screen six and the time. We saw them supposedly head down the emergency exit at 10:18, right?

"Right."

"Well, let's watch from 10:18, and you tell me what you see at 10:19." At that time, there was no activity, only a few Emergency and medical staff chatting and smoking, when suddenly, to the one side, there was a swift flash of light.

"Let me guess, no point in backing this up and doing a frame-by-frame breakdown, because I'm still not going to see anything?"

"Unfortunately, that's all we have, Detective. In all my years, I have never seen anything like this."

"You're telling me, responds Detective Ramos. "I do have this figured out, though."

"You're kidding. What are you talking about?" asks Humphreys.

"Are you a fan of Marvel comics, you know, the Superheroes, Batman, Spiderman? I think we're dealing with a Superhero here. Think about it. She used her x-ray vision to knock the cameras out. She flew out of the Emergency exit. I just haven't figured out the whole dog angle yet. I think I can sell that theory to my Lieutenant. He's a big Superheroes fan."

"Well, at least you are finding some humor in this whole whacky episode, Detective.

"In any event, Mr. Humphrey, I still would like a copy of those tapes with those times so I can send them to our own CIS video techs to see if they can decipher anything from those blurred flash outs."

"No problem, Detective, we'll get them right over to the station house."

"I need to collect my thoughts and review my notes for a few minutes. Would you mind clearing the room, as I'm sure you guys could use a break?"

"By all means, Detective."

Ramos rewinds some of the footage he has just viewed, shaking his head as he stares at the frame-by-frame view. Thinking back to those boys down at the river and their statement about the dog and the figure at the top of the hill, and again nothing was found on any of the surrounding cameras. 'How is any of this possible? Nurse Rosita, on the surface, would have no obvious motivation to lie, and she was very positive in describing the sequence of events. She obviously saw a person and dog and the whole business with the victim's direct recovery. Something or someone absolutely arrived here last night, but what's the connection to this victim? She shows up with that frigging dog when Jane Doe washes up on the Brooklyn shoreline, and now a month later, her appearance resuscitates the victim. You can't make this up, and how do I explain any of this to the Lieutenant and my unit?'

Slowly shifting his train of thoughts, there is still one bright light: Jane Doe lying in her bed. 'It's time to shift my focus.' Now Detective Ramos has interviewed all kinds of characters over his many years on the force, many of which had suffered some form of shock or traumatic event and subsequently experienced temporary amnesia or immediate memory loss, so he feels very confident to separate what may be real from anyone pretending to be suffering with some form of amnesia. He read the preliminary report from the resident psychiatrist, which stated that it was still too early to give any diagnosis as to the extent or depth of amnesia. The shrink has decided to have a series of sessions with the patient to assess her mental condition more accurately. Medically, while there were still more tests to be administered, there was no obvious indication of any neurological damage. With all this background information, Detective Ramos sauntered down to Jane Doe's room to begin his first interrogation.

Detective Ramos and Jane Doe

IT'S LATE MORNING now, and the attending nurse is on her way out of the room and explains to Ramos that the patient is quite weak and that she was able to bathe her and wash and groom her hair, but she is still quite frail. Ramos tells her he won't be long or antagonistic with the patient. As he enters the room, she is propped up, lying on the bed, staring out the window deep in her own thoughts, searching for any answers as to how she lost a month of her life and now is in this hospital surrounded by total strangers.

"Excuse me, Miss, I am Detective Ramos from the 69th precinct. If you feel up to it, I would like to ask you a few questions, so maybe we can understand your situation and maybe get to the bottom of what happened to you and hopefully return you to your family or loved ones."

Taking a very caring and encouraging tone, the detective is hoping to disarm the young lady in distress. Seeing her again, but now in quite a different condition, he is immediately taken with her natural beauty. Long shimmering sable-colored hair flowing down past her shoulders, wide almond-shaped brown berry eyes and the smooth pure olive complexion and somber smile were almost intoxicating. He suddenly feels like the one that has been disarmed by her innocent expression and the sense of vulnerability that envelopes her persona. Waving off his own mixed feelings of attraction and compassion for someone who appears to be a lost soul searching for her own identity, he refocuses his train of thought.

"I've been told you speak Spanish as well as English?"

"Yes," she responds.

"Would you mind translating in Spanish just a few of the words you hear on the television, as well as you can? Don't worry if you make any mistakes." The Detective takes the TV remote and turns up the volume on the TV set above her bed. She fluently repeats almost word for word, everything stated on the TV in her distinct accent.

Ramos quickly interrupts, "That's impressive." His rationale for asking this curious first question was a means to determine what her dialect is because he has encountered just about every nationality, having worked so many years in the city, and now it is quite evident to him that she is clearly from South America, possibly Colombia, maybe Brazil. Thinking fast now, he is ruling out that she is Puerto Rican or was born here in the States, a process of elimination without being obvious.

"I know the Psychiatrist and some of the doctors have already asked you a lot of questions already, so I will try and not be repetitive. Can you recall any of the living conditions from your childhood? If you lived in a city, countryside, or village? If you were rich, poor, middle class, brothers, sisters, anything about your parents?"

As the patient's expression clearly turns gloomy, she responds quietly. "No, I am trying so hard to remember anything. I look in this mirror the nurse gave me, and I can't recall anything about my past or present. Can you understand how upsetting that is? I don't even know who I am, where I came from, what happened to me . . . nothing . . . Nothing." As her eyes begin to well with tears, Ramos, despite his hardened nature from all he has experienced, is moved by her obvious despair.

"At this point, can I ask you just one or two more questions?" She nodded in agreement.

"You may not be aware of it yet, but the medical staff mentioned to me that you have some older scars on your lower back." Her eyes widen as she struggles now to feel her back.

"No, don't worry, everything is fine, and they are well healed and quite old, nothing to be concerned about. My apologies for upsetting you, but what I am trying to get at is that sometimes in a dream or a fleeting thought, we very briefly see a flash of some traumatic event, like a car crash, a fire, or an explosion of some kind, maybe the death of a loved one, or a brutally physical encounter of some kind. Have you ever had any inklings of anything along those lines where you may have been harmed?"

Shaking her head with a somewhat confused expression on her face, she quietly says no.

"I know some of these questions probably seem off the wall to you, but we are just trying to fit the pieces of your puzzle together for us based on what little we know about you, so please bear with me. One last question, which I'm sure may seem strange to you right now, but do you ever recall having a pet, like a dog or had a close relationship with any kind of a religious person?"

Somewhat put off by the odd nature of this last line of questioning and clearly tired, the exasperated young beauty replies, "Religious person?" She pauses. "Tell you what, Detective, I've already tried to reach out to God for help in restoring my memory." Her speech stammers. "What happened . . . send me a clue . . . how . . . why me . . . but so far . . . nothing . . . just another lost soul at sea, I guess." Her voice trails off.

As her demeanor has completely soured, Detective Ramos realizes he has overstayed his time and is not going to get anything more from her. "Well, I can see you are tired. I would like to leave my card here on the table should any memory flashbacks return or due to any treatment by the fine medical staff here. I will keep in touch with your doctors and stop by from time to time."

The Detective closes his small, dog-eared notepad and pauses, sensing his questions have only caused her more anguish. Yet, at the same time, there is this other feeling of kinship that he can't seem to shake off. Before he leaves, he says, "I know everything may seem hopeless now, but you have a lot of people working on your case, and you don't know anything about me, but I will get some answers . . . for the both of us . . . I am one hell of a Detective."

Detective Ramos and Chris

PRESENT DAY (mid-September 2017)

CHRIS HAD ALREADY checked with his buddy at the DA's office if he would consider checking out this whole missing person thing and if there is any connection to Marisa. His old college buddy couldn't offer anything more than what he had discovered in that newspaper article. He did relay to Chris that based on the information they had in the system, there was a special note that anyone with any information really should contact Detective Ramos rather than the Missing Persons division. He passed the location of the detective's station along with his contact information along to Chris. Chris headed into the city on this warm September morning, the same day he was supposed to meet Marisa at the entrance of Central Park Zoo. Chris stopped at the central desk in the police station and asked if he could meet with Detective Ramos. The female Sergeant at the desk asked what it was in reference to, and he explained the reason for his meeting. The Sergeant hesitated for a moment as she was about to brush him off, and she asked Chris, "Did you say this is about a Marisa Flores?"

"Yes, that's right," Chris responded.

"Would you take a seat over in the waiting area and let me see if he's available?"

Sitting in the waiting area and watching all the various types of individuals coming and going, Chris is starting to second guess his request, but his curiosity about Marisa overrides his anxiety.

After about ten minutes, Chris is summoned by the Desk Sergeant, and Detective Haggerty arrives to accompany Chris to Detective Ramos's office. They arrive upstairs among an array of desks, people scurrying about in all directions, some in uniform, others mostly in plain clothes. There is an abundance of two-person conversations, others drinking their coffee buried deep in their computer screens or documents, as he is directed to this small conference room.

Once inside the small conference room, he is greeted by Detective Ramos. "Have a seat, Mr.?"

"Reardon, Chris Reardon," Chris responds.

"Very nice to meet you, Mr. Reardon. I am Detective Frank Ramos. Also joining us is my partner in crime, Detective

Haggerty. I understand you requested to speak with us about Ms. Flores. Is that correct?"

"Yep, I really didn't want to take a lot of your time, all I . . ."

"Excuse me for a second here, Mr. Reardon, but would you mind if I ask you a few questions first?"

Chris is taken back a little. "Uh, sure."

"Would you mind telling us why you have an interest in knowing about Ms. Flores and just how did you meet Ms. Flores . . . and when was that, exactly?"

Chris, in his usual confident manner, "No problem. I met Marisa, Ms. Flores, at a party last week on Saturday night, which she attended as a waitress. During the course of the party, we met, chatted a little and as I'm sure you are all quite aware, she is very attractive, so I took the opportunity to ask her for a date, and she agreed. As a matter of fact, we are meeting today by the entrance of the Central Park Zoo for lunch."

"Okay, then why would you be here and feel you have some need to check her out?" responds Detective Ramos.

"Well, I guess this is a little embarrassing, but you know how social media is these days and how easy it is to check anyone out? So being a cautious guy, especially since we planned to meet, I googled her, and upon further investigation, I discovered she may have been a missing person just a few months ago. Or, hopefully, I am mistaken."

"Well, that all makes sense to me. Let me ask you just a few more questions before we get into Ms. Flores's background," the Detective replies. "Have you ever been married or are married now? Not that any of this is an issue for us, but maybe we just want to check you out a little."

"No, I'm definitely single, Detective," Chris sighs.

"I sense some disappointment, a good-looking, seemingly successful young man like yourself. Have you ever had any bad experiences . . . You know what I mean . . . any trouble with any women in your recent past or previously?"

"Quite frankly, Detective, just the opposite. I lost someone I was very close with a little more than a year ago."

"Sorry to hear . . . if it's not too difficult, would you mind sharing just the generalities as to the circumstances, again, just for our information."

Chris takes another big sigh and begins. "I was engaged to this wonderful, lovely young woman, and she was killed in a car accident. And that's pretty much it. Now you know why I have not been this big player in the field with the ladies, as any dates have been just about non-existent since that time."

"Truly sorry, Mr. Reardon. I think we have all the information we need, unless you have something, Haggerty?"

"Nah, I'm good, Frank. He seems like a legit guy."

"Once I explain Ms. Flores's circumstances, I think you will better understand why we wanted to learn a little about you before we started sharing, because this is a unique situation.

Now they have Chris's undivided attention as his somber mood has quickly transitioned to a rather apprehensive status. "As strange as this may seem as to what I am about to tell you, Ms. Flores's case as a missing person is still very much an open case."

"I don't understand," Chris replies inquisitively.

"Obviously, we all know she is alive and well and where she lives, works, and so on; the fascinating aspect of this case is . . . we don't know anything about her, where she came from, no known past . . . as a matter of fact, Marisa Flores is not her real name."

"Whoa, what am I getting myself into here?" Chris is now clearly alarmed.

"I know this all sounds a little crazy, but let me alleviate some of your concerns," replies Detective Ramos. "The reason we don't have any answers to any of those questions is because when we discovered her in critical condition down by the East River some five to six months ago, she was unconscious and had suffered a severe head wound resulting in her remaining in a sustained coma for about a month. She . . ." the detective pauses, "for whatever reason, has a miraculous recovery and awakens. However, not without one major setback, she experiences full-on amnesia. Subsequently, she was thoroughly tested for any neurological problems, which thankfully were all negative. Following that process, she was treated for her amnesia, not only at Lennox Hill but by some of the top neuropsychologists and psychiatrists in the city, unfortunately, with no real success. The good news is she is a perfectly healthy individual in all respects. Moreover, it turns out after all that psychological testing mumbo jumbo, the prevailing profile for Ms. Flores is that she was a well-educated individual during some point in her life as she is quite knowledgeable about many subjects and tested in the top ten percent aptitude-wise."

"Wait, you're telling me she is a highly educated woman but doesn't know where she even went to any school, grew up or where she was born? How is that possible?"

"Chris. Since we are getting into a lot of personal information here on both sides, we will be fully transparent about everything we know about her past. If we knew the answer to that one, we could wrap this whole case up."

Chris's mind is whirling, trying to digest and assess concurrently whether this is someone he should get involved with as the details surrounding the background of Marisa's past continue to be revealed.

"Can we back up for a second?" Chris inquires. "The whole business about her body being found on the East Riverfront. What was that all about? Was she robbed, attacked, or worse," he pauses, "raped?"

Detective Ramos interrupts. "No, thankfully, she was spared that calamity. Everything came back negative on that front."

"Could she be married? Have children? There's absolutely no evidence of anything from her past?" Chris asks.

"That's pretty much where we are at," replies Ramos warily. "And over these four to five months, no new clues? She has had no memory flashbacks of any kind?"

"No, she is being treated on a weekly basis by a specially appointed shrink to monitor her progress, and he keeps us appraised of any changes or new developments."

"Unbelievable!" Chris sits back in his chair, dumbfounded, and totally befuddled as to how to proceed. Never in his wildest dreams of possibilities had he ever thought this would be the outcome of his somewhat frivolous investigation.

"I can see you are having second thoughts about following through with your initial intentions to meet Marisa. Let me share one theory, and it is just that. From all indications and opinions from all the medical professionals, we believe she was most likely born and raised somewhere in Colombia, South America. Given her demeanor, personality traits, and physical characteristics, our profile theory is this. As you are probably aware, that is a country riddled with many large cartel organizations.

"Our speculation, and it is just that, she may have been the daughter, niece, or granddaughter of possibly some major Cartel leader, and at some point, in her youth, or as a very young adult, there may have been a major confrontation with one of the rival organizations, and these can be brutal. All unimaginable forms of cruelty hurled at one another. Assuming she does have a relationship with a Cartel leader that is more than likely dead now, someone from the Cartel sought a safe haven for her and brought her to this country, most likely under some alias, which is why we can't trace her entry into this country. This is something they do in similar cases, and with the money they provided for her, she continued her new life in this country. That would also explain why no family members claimed her when we reached out in the public sector. However, and this is all my own conjecture, someone from that rival cartel eventually, more than likely by accident, discovered her real identity and that she was alive in this country. They may be the ones who might have attempted to finish her off, but fortunately for her, they screwed that up as she is very much alive and living a new life in the big city."

Chris, listening attentively the whole time, replies, "This entire saga is like something out of one of those cheesy B movies or mini-series."

"Like I said, Chris, a pretty big theory, but some aspects of our investigation are following up on some definite leads in that direction."

"Uh, you are forgetting a few other details, Frank," detective Haggerty now interrupts.

"Oh, yeah, just for your information, Chris. Let me fill in a few more blanks for you with respect to her name and how she got that job. Over the course of her treatment with the whole range of psychologists, shrinks, testing, etc., in their attempts to help her recover any memories and my own interest in her case, we kind of developed this relationship. You know, father-daughter, uncle-niece, whatever . . ."

Detective Haggerty chuckles to himself in the corner and interrupts, "He's got this thing for her, and none of us can quite put our finger on it."

"Alright, Haggerty, no, nothing like that. I just feel very protective, plus I have a vested interest in her case. We stay in touch, and she has a 24/7 emergency alert device should she encounter any strange characters or find herself in some potentially dangerous situation." Chris tries to say something, but the Detective continues. "And in addition to myself, she has a godmother who has kind of adopted her. Her name is Rosita Flores, she was the nurse at Lennox Hill that spent a lot of time with Marisa on her night shift, and they developed this close relationship. Once it was clear she was physically and mentally healthy enough to be released, the problem was what authority we turn her over to, and not for nothing this young lady still has no identity, money, clothes, or family. We have a walking, talking, very present, missing person.

"I talked with the Feds, and Immigration can't deport her. We don't know, in fact, if she was born here or in a foreign country, so where would you send her? So, between Rosita and my own connections with the mayor's office and Social Services, we got her a special visa status. Rosita offered to take her in with her and is in the process of having her last name adopted to Flores, hence Marisa Flores. We pulled a few more strings and got her a job via the City's Social Services, working for an upscale catering firm as a waitress to earn some income and then take it from there. Now you have her whole story. Any more questions, Chris?"

As both detectives, Ramos, and Haggerty, are looking at one another and chuckling, Chris is staring at the floor, speechless and kind of shaking his head.

"This is all too fucking crazy. She seems like a perfectly healthy individual, like she has it all together. There was nothing out of the ordinary, spoke two languages, I picked up on that, and she came across as a bright, happy person."

"And she is, Chris, quite bright, as I mentioned previously about her aptitude. She may have amnesia, but she is one smart cookie. Don't kid yourself and can be quite sassy once you really get to know her, but that's up to you, pal."

Chris, still rolling the chronology of Marisa's past in his head, says, "You know, Detective, all my instincts tell me to walk away, but maybe I could use a little adventure in my life, and her situation is really out there, so why not?"

Chris pauses, and the Detective interjects, "And she is quite beautiful."

"Yes, there is that" Chris responds with a grin. "One last thing, Detective. Your little Cartel theory, if it holds any validity, then she could still be in some degree of danger should her new identity be revealed somehow."

"You got it, and don't think we aren't going to check your background in full because even though we had this nice conversation today, you would make a great decoy for them, coming across as this curious, naive American businessman who just happens to want some date out of the blue. You just could be the first break in this case." Chris, shaking his head and smiling broadly, bids a quick goodbye to the two Detectives.

"So, what's your verdict, Chris."

Chris turns before passing through the door. "Innocent, and I'm going for it. This should be one helluva date!"

"Fair enough, and I wish you well, but remember we will be around, and if there's any funny stuff, you will be hearing from me personally," replies Detective Ramos.

As Chris heads out of the office, Ramos shoots a look at detective Haggerty. "Whadda you think?"

"He's alright. He probably just wants to get laid."

"You falling for that nice Irish choir boy shit?"

"Come on, Frank, we can't suspect everybody or is it because he wants to date your little girl?" Haggerty says, getting his little dig in.

"Funny. It's that whole Wall Street thing, and he is definitely in that category. I don't trust any of them. Put a plain clothes man on him for this date. Also, let's do that full background work up on him. I want to know what this guy had for breakfast."

Chris walks quickly to his car as it is nearing the time of his date with Marisa by Central Park Zoo. Thinking to himself, is he crazy for following up on this date after everything he has heard about her past, but there is that inescapable haunting feeling that he personally needs to know more about her. What is this mystifying connection?

The Date

CHRIS MAKES HIS way through the maze of people towards the Central Park Zoo entrance on this breezy, warm September afternoon. As he approaches the entrance, he catches his first glimpse of Marisa since the party. He pauses and just marvels at her natural beauty and athletic build, coupled now with this mysterious past. Is she just an innocent caught in some one-off criminal incident or a Cartel figure who may be capable of all kinds of previous corrupt deeds and or insidious criminal acts? Chris shakes all these potential negative thoughts from his head as he watches Marisa innocently chatting with some young child and her mother. She is dressed casually but fashionably for her age, and Chris is doing his best to subdue his anxiety as well as enthusiasm as he moves across from her, smiling.

Marisa looks up and sees Chris. Their eyes meet, igniting that instant connection between them. It is undeniable and magical, which neither of them understands or can explain; but there it is. Marisa breaks the ice. "you are a man of your word and really were serious about meeting me for lunch."

"There was never any question," replies Chris as he swiftly moves over to her side. "If you have the time, I thought we'd take a little stroll through the park on our way to lunch and take advantage of this beautiful weather," Chris suggests.

"Works for me," replies Marisa. "You know this is fairly brazen on my part, as I don't know anything about you, other than I guess you live somewhere down by the Jersey shore."

As they saunter down one of those meadow-like paths filled with an assortment of greenery, flowering shrubs and the swishing hum of the leaves swaying in the trees above their heads, Chris catches a whiff of that familiar intoxicating perfume that he knows so well. Quickly putting that memory aside, he responds to Marisa. "Well, I work in midtown in wealth management."

Their banter continues as they follow the winding path through the park. The more they walk, talk, and exchange those fleeting glances to really absorb the other's persona, the more they become engaged and comforted with the emerging chemistry that is enshrouding them.

As they make their way along the winding path, they come across a series of huge craggy rocks, and Marisa, feeling much more comfortable with Chris's presence, decides to be a little playful by throwing out a challenge to Chris. "Let's see just what kind of shape you're in; I bet I can beat you to the top of that rounded boulder."

"You're on," replies Chris. As they both start to scale the various nooks and crannies of the staggered rocky hill, Chris is somewhat amazed at Marisa's athleticism, speed, and the ease with which she climbs but soon catches just a glimpse of a tattooed wing above the left hip of Marisa as her clothes stretch out in her attempt to maneuver the staggered rocky terrain. They both arrive on the top of the rounded boulder laughing and carefully make their way back down to the path before them. Joking and teasing each other's athletic skills, Chris spies a nearby bench and suggests they sit for a second while they catch their breath. As the September breeze grows stronger and heavier clouds roll in, there is a hint of one of those September storms brewing.

Chris staring at the captivating Marisa. "Can I ask you a little personal question?"

Marisa, smiling and soaking in every feature on Chris's face, shifts her demeanor immediately at Chris's request. Sensing she is going to be entering unknown territory that could change the tenor of their whole meeting thus far. Marisa hadn't planned to get into this level of conversation until they had spent a lot more time together. She felt it was way too premature to reveal any part of that unfathomable, deep, dark secret that haunts her soul daily and the inner turmoil she has experienced with her memory. On the other hand, she has had this pervasive burning desire to unburden herself of this conscious presence, and it could only be shared with Chris, as he may be the only person on the planet that could help her. About a week following her initial recovery, Marisa experienced an inexplicable event that most likely was the source of her phantom memory.

She was staring out the hospital window around twilight in the evening when suddenly a beautiful bright white dove with blue-tipped wings alighted on the small ledge outside her window. Somewhat shocked by the sudden appearance of such a gorgeous creature just sitting outside her window beside her, Marisa started to feel a little edgy. She then got this eerie feeling that the dove was acting like she knew Marisa and literally fixated on the movement of Marisa's eyes, following the path of her sight diligently.

Thinking to herself, 'For God's sake, it's a dove. You want to have a staring contest? Let's do it.' The more she stared at the dove, the more transfixed she became at its presence, and before she knew it, the dove arose from its perch on the ledge and, with its beautiful wings spread wide, hovered outside her window and whether she imagined it or not; the dove started to grow more luminous and larger all the while with its spanned wings. The incandescent aura glowing around the dove grew brighter and larger as its brilliance would have blinded any other person within sight of its image, but Marisa was already in a hypnotic state by this time. Without any warning, the dazzling aura encircling the dove started to rise rapidly in the evening sky and transpose into a star-like essence, ethereal, glistening, otherworldly, higher, and higher until it evaporated into the creeping darkness of the starlit night.

When Marisa recovered from her trance-like hypnosis, she quickly looked around the room and at the entrance to her room, but all activities seemed perfectly routine. What had just happened? Was it real? Was it all in her mind due to the amnesia and all the recent testing starting to affect her brain? She sat in stunned silence for several minutes now wondering if her sanity was going to be an issue; how could she possibly even mention this bizarre incident?

As she sat quietly in her hospital bed, quite unnerved and upset by what she had just witnessed that night, an overwhelming urge to rest and sleep overcame her, and she just thought to herself maybe this was all somehow part of the amnesia recovery process that her brain must go through for her to regain her memory. She finally laid her head down to rest and fell fast asleep, as if she had been placed under a mystical spell.

That night, as she slipped into a deep, deep state of sleep, her memory bank started to flood with new images. It was as if her mind was being streamed by an internet feed from a huge data storage device. Years of memories . . . images of a woman . . . a man . . . locations from all over the world . . . a torrent of emotions that hit her memory bank like a tidal wave. As the weeks of medical and psychological testing and conversations continued, Marisa never mentioned any of what was now locked in her memory as she was trying to understand it. Moreover, she felt mentioning any of it made no sense, and the medical professionals might think she had some serious psychiatric issues. She locked this whole episode away because even though it was the only memory she possessed; Marisa also realized this was not something she personally experienced but now had become part of who she was. How could she possibly make sense of or attempt to explain any of this to anyone? Until she saw Chris that night at the party.

The more Marisa ruminated about this memory and the people involved, it started to take a life of its own in her mind as she specifically obsessed about the woman and extraordinary man she was romantically involved with. Marisa was able to recall every small detail and conversation that took place between the two lovers. Either consciously or subconsciously, over time, she started to identify with this woman in many respects and subsequently adopted her personality, living habits, mannerisms, clothes, and the way she wore her hair. In many ways, this woman who went by the name of Theresa was inhabiting her memory and started to take over her own persona.

Marisa realizes that once she releases any little detail about these memories, it has the potential to shatter any chance of having any kind of relationship with anyone who knew her, to say nothing of how explosive this information may be perceived by any persons listening to what she reveals. So, with great trepidation, she decides to move forward, but swiftly changes her tactic.

She decides to take charge of the conversation. For the first time since the occasion of their meeting, Marisa takes a formal tone. "Okay, but first, let me ask you a personal question."

"Fair enough," replies Chris.

"From all those good-looking young ladies that I saw at the party that night, some of whom you must have known or were clearly well-to-do professional ladies, why would you seek out a working waitress and total stranger?"

Chris has always prided himself on being quick on his feet in business and social situations but quickly realized he needed to give a somewhat nebulous answer without giving away his own deeper intentions. "I just got a thing for attractive women in uniforms," trying to be humorous and joke his way out of Marisa's more seriously posed query.

Marisa wasn't buying it and pressed him further. "Seriously, Chris, believe it or not, this is important to me." There it was her question just hanging in the air.

"Okay, truth be told, I had hoped to meet a young lady I had recently made the acquaintance of, but she never showed. My expectations had been kind of shattered, and I was just starting to drown my disappointment in more drinks when I caught my first real glimpse of you serving drinks, and what can I say? I was immediately attracted. Honestly, I can't give you a specific reason, but hey, I'm just a guy."

Marisa, still in a very pensive, solemn mood, said, "So, then you decided to seek me out that night, which sounds a little desperate, but I get it. Yet, as I recall, when we met, you said you had this unmistakable feeling that we had met before or had a mutual friend or something like that. Don't get me wrong, I get a lot of lines like that, but you came across as being very sincere and honest when you approached me. Can you share who it was that I may have reminded you of?"

Chris, betraying his own need to unburden himself of why he really wanted to meet Marisa that night, replies, "You know you meet so many people, and I guess I was just mistaken, maybe I did have too much to drink that night. I honestly don't recall what I was thinking, other than that, yes, I found you to be very attractive, and I just wanted to meet you. Maybe you're right, I was just getting desperate," again trying to feign some humor in his response to Marisa.

"You know lying is not really your forte. I really think you had someone in mind, but let's not get all hung up on that right now. So, what was your personal question?" Marisa was now somewhat disappointed and annoyed that Chris was avoiding a potential opening for her.

"While we were scaling that rocky hill, I happened to catch something of a tattoo on your lower back; I was just curious what it was?"

"You mean that dove that I have just above my butt cheek? Were you just checking out my behind, or are you really interested in knowing what my tattoo looks like."

"No, seriously, I saw just a glimpse and was curious what it is." She stands up and tugs down just a few inches on the side of her capri' slacks, and sure enough, there is a white dove and one that is very familiar. Chris smiles, but his mind is racing with the heavy remembrance of another almost identical dove that graced the lower back of Theresa.

As Chris sits back on the bench, he is still somewhat astonished by the similarity in appearance of the dove and its precise placement, as it was a very special occasion when Theresa first got that tattoo. It was the night that he first told her he loved her, and both having too much to drink, had passed a tattoo lounge on the way back to their hotel while on a romantic holiday. It was at that moment Theresa announced her intention to get that tattoo. While he sat at her side while the tattoo was being inked on her backside, she explained to Chris that the dove was her favorite bird because it was a symbol of peace, love, and spirituality and that, should they ever get married, she would get an adjoining dove during their honeymoon, "Because Chris, doves' mate for life." They both laughed joyously that night; it was one of Chris's favorite memories of their time together. Marisa, sensing Chris's bewilderment, decides to seize the moment because she knows . . . she knows only too well what must be running through his mind.

Moving close, inches away from his face, Marisa asks, "Now do you remember who I remind you of, Chris? Was it the way I carried myself, something I said, something in my features, or the way I looked at you when we first met, or what we both felt that night? This is all no accident, Chris. You know me, and I know you."

Stunned by her declaration, Chris tries to draw back in his seat, but Marisa is committed now and pushes the envelope. She leans into him and slowly reaches across to caress him. "Maybe this will help your memory," and lays a full-lipped, deep lingering sensuous kiss on him.

Chris is dazed by her startling move but lost in the moment of her kiss and how the familiarity of that kiss floods his brain with so many memories of Theresa. They both slowly lean back, staring deep into one another's eyes, trying to grasp the sublime experience that just took place.

Marisa is bubbling over internally with a torrent of emotions . . . desire . . . hope . . . yearning but yielding to the greatest need for some hint of recognition on Chris's part. Chris is reeling and trying to reign in his own inner feelings as well but wait a minute. 'What is she saying? What does she mean, I know her?'

Marisa can't deny the exuberance she experienced in that kiss and a weird sense of familiarity at the same time, and now is beyond herself with excitement at the prospect of confronting Chris with all that she knows. "Chris, remember the dove tattoo, San Francisco, dinner on the pier at Ghirardelli Square, the first time . . . you told me you loved me."

Chris recoils, stunned, glaring at Marisa. "What are you talking about? How can you know? Who are you?"

Now shifting in her tone from excitement and daring to an almost begging manner, Marisa says, "Chris, please just listen. Please bear with me while I try to explain. I know this all sounds crazy, but you are the only person I can trust. Who will understand what I am about to share? Only you can help me, please, Chris. Just give me a few minutes to try and explain, because I don't understand any of this either."

The darkening clouds above have turned stormy, and the wind is blowing the swaying branches and swirling leaves throughout the park as the strolling populace starts to move swiftly now for cover. There's a rumble of thunder and some distant flashes of lightning as a few large drops of rain start to hit the ground. Chris slowly rises from the bench, lost somewhere between disbelief at what he heard and astonishment. Staring down at Marisa as now he can see she is struggling to reach out and get some response from him, Marisa, in desperation, finally relents and blurts out, "It's Theresa, Chris, Theresa. I know everything about her, and about you."

With that pronouncement, the wind, rain and overall clamor of the storm have now moved directly above their heads as the rain falls at a rapid pace, pelting both Marisa and Chris. Chris is staggered at her declaration and is smoldering with emotions as to how to respond to the fact that Marisa could never dare to claim to have known his Theresa. Regaining his composure so that he doesn't go off on Marisa in a rage, he realizes that this is someone that has suffered an obvious unfortunate trauma that has clearly affected her mind. He decides to take a more reasoned, compassionate response.

"Marisa, I'm sorry, but I am leaving. I have no idea what you are talking about. I think you need to get help. I just can't deal with this. Whether you realize it or not, you have said some very crazy but hurtful things, and I can't be with anyone like you."

As the rain drenches the two forlorn souls in the park, Chris starts to walk away as Marisa, in her anguish, cries out, "Chris, just listen, please give me a chance. You are my only hope. I need you." The tears fall down her cheeks in concert with the rain. Before Chris gets too far, Marisa stands and shouts in the pouring rain, "I will always be by your side."

Chris stops dead in his tracks. Shocked, dazed, and speechless by what he just heard. Chris stammers out, "No, no, that's impossible. You need to go away. This is crazy. I have to get outta here." Chris races out of there, running through the park back to his car. Marisa, weeping and distraught, slowly makes her way back to her apartment in midtown.

As Chris makes his way through the dragging mid-town traffic, half talking and thinking to himself, "What the fuck is the matter with me? I should have listened to that detective. She must have suffered something horrible in her past. She is damaged goods. I don't want any part of that crazy broad."

Finally, he makes his way out of the city and heads back down the highway towards his Jersey shore home in what has now turned into a tempestuous September storm. Chilled by the soaking wet clothes and shuddering at times at the thought of some of Marisa's comments, he is now starting to focus more and more on all the events of that afternoon, thinking them through and replaying them one by one in his mind.

Arielle's Challenge

AS CHRIS GETS closer to home after rewinding the events of this afternoon, he slowly realizes how much Marisa knew about Theresa, their relationship, about that night in San Francisco, and most of all, Theresa's last whispered words from beyond.

Moreover, there was no denying that before their whole date blew up, he was having a terrific time, and there was that irrefutable, powerful, intense connection between the two of them. How is it possible that this beautiful, supposedly half-dead woman of South American origin washed up along the East River in Brooklyn months after Theresa's death and now has this inconceivable connection to Theresa? Still mumbling, cursing to himself, and disheveled, Chris pulls into his garage, bounds up the stairs to his study to make himself a tall drink, and stares out the window at the horrific storm he just had to plow through all the way home. Stewing with all kinds of emotions, confused, and dismayed, he catches a glimpse of a figure standing in his enclosed patio area out by the ocean. He thinks to himself, 'What now? Who is this?' He slowly walks towards the patio area and soon recognizes the familiar figure. Looking more angelic than in any of their previous meetings, Arielle stands in a long flowing white robe with the hood resting on the back of her neck; she acknowledges Chris's presence.

"Perfect, just perfect. Come on in; it's wacky Wednesday. All the crazies are out today, so join the party." With that, a smiling Arielle and Abbey approach Chris as he crashes into one of his big lounge chairs in the den near his gas fireplace that he had just turned on to take the chill off him and his damp clothes.

"Tell me, did you just float in, arrive on a falling star, or am I having another frigging flashback hallucination? I know I'm not drunk yet because I've only started on my first drink."

"What's the matter, Chris? Rough day?"

"Rough day? No, maybe surreal, mind-blowing, outrageous, take your pick! Let me recap my day. I went to the city for what I believed would be," Chris hesitates a second, "an interesting date with a very beautiful woman. Truth is, in an odd way, you are responsible because I met this woman as a result of you not showing up at that party, we discussed last month. Anyway, before I met this lovely woman today, I had checked her out on social media, and I needed to confirm my findings about her background in, of all places, a police station. Now, right off the bat, that's a red flag if there ever was one, but does that stop me from checking her out? No, not me. I'm curious George.

"I meet with the detective who explains to me that this nice young lady I have a date with this afternoon washed up on the East River in Brooklyn and was practically dead." Arielle is expressionless and just observes and listens attentively to Chris's every word as he rants on.

Chris is now pacing the floor as he is getting amped up, recalling the day's events. "I'm only warming up. This whole story gets a lot better. Turns out this young lady was in a coma, recovers and has total amnesia. Are you frigging kidding me? She has no idea who she is or where she came from.

"They don't even know if she is from this country because they are pretty sure she is Colombian and that she may have some possible drug cartel connections. But does any of that stop me from meeting my appointed date? Nah, no way, this is going to be an adventure, I'm thinking. I've been stuck in this rut in my life, going nowhere. I need to meet someone new and exciting. I need to change things up in my life, so I'm going for it. Boy, did I hit the mother load?

"The date starts out great. She is gorgeous and seems quite happy that we are meeting. I suggest a walk in the park before lunch, and we are having a nice engaging conversation, getting to know one another. Everything was going quite well. I decided to ask a question about some tattoo I happen to catch a glimpse of, and then all hell breaks loose. She starts making all these wild accusations, statements, that we know one another already, that I am the only person that can help her, that somehow, she intimately knows someone that was very close to me and with that, this horrendous storm appears out of nowhere, and we both get soaked in the process."

"What happened then?" queries Arielle.

"I got the hell out of there. I mean, come on, we just really met, trying to get to know one another. Yes, she is very attractive. As a matter of fact, there was even this kiss that she sprung on me. Talk about erratic behavior, but yeah, that part was remarkable.

"That was my day, and now you're here and now . . ." Chris stops and gets ready to prepare another drink for himself. "Wait. Where are my manners? Would you like something, vodka, scotch, a sprite, or should I say a spirit?" Chris is amused at his own witticism. "I have maybe a thousand questions, like what are you doing here and just who are you?"

"Fair enough. I guess it is time we drop all pretense, but by way of my explanation to you, can I just ask you a few questions about your meeting with this obviously distraught soul?"

"Sure, fire away," Chris responds, as the liquor starts to restore his confidence and some semblance of sanity.

"This young lady has a name?"

"Yes, Yes, Marisa."

"And she claimed that she knew you and that somehow you knew her from some past experience?"

"Correctamundo," Chris replies sarcastically.

"She also stated that you had some knowledge or key to her past that would enable her to understand whatever it was that was troubling her?"

"Yeah, that's pretty close to what she was inferring."

"One last question. You said she mentioned that she knew someone who was very close to you. Did she happen to give you a name?"

Chris's cocky, wise-cracking nature shifts and grows more serious, as well as very puzzled about where Arielle is going with this last line of questioning.

"She said she knew Theresa, my former fiancée, whom I loved dearly and is now deceased."

There is a dead silence between the two of them now. Chris is staring at Arielle and that barely visible aura that now seems to constantly illuminate her appearance, making her appear even more beautiful than when they first met. Chris breaks the stalemate and says in a calculated tone, "But you know all of this already, don't you?"

"Yes, Chris, I just wanted to hear your version of the day's events and gain some insight as to how you feel about everything that just happened. As a matter of fact, I was there the whole time."

Chris, stunned, almost drops his drink. "You were there? In the park? And you heard everything that was said between Marisa and me?"

"Yes."

"How is that possible? Okay, I'm done. Just who are you, some kind of spiritual messenger? And why are you here, spending time with me? I would think there are a lot more important matters than you intruding in my social life. You know, pandemics, Middle East peace, world poverty, social unrest, I think you know the list. Wait a minute. I get it. You're my Guardian Angel, but why would you make an actual physical appearance multiple times now and for some ordinary Joe like me?"

"Well, Chris, you're half right, and for the sake of simplicity, if you want to call me an angel, that's fine . . . but I'm not your Guardian Angel . . . I am Marisa's?"

"What! You're here for Marisa? Then why are you talking to me? She's the one who needs help, not me. Christ, she needs a caretaker."

Arielle, in her sincerest tone, attempts to make Chris understand, as Abbey is perched directly at her feet while she stands. "You see, there is this well-designed strategy from above that requires Marisa's and your joint participation. I was tasked with the assignment to facilitate the development of your relationship with Marisa because I am her guardian and messenger. Subsequently, it was necessary that I intervene in your social life, as you put it and establish a kind of relationship with you by way of all these meetings on Marisa's behalf."

"You're telling me that you and I have been doing this little dance to somehow benefit Marisa?"

"Come on, Chris, think about what you just told me. How did you meet Marisa? Remember, I never showed up at that party."

"You're telling me this whole thing is some kind of setup?"

"A plan, Chris, a simple plan for the two of you to meet."

"Matchmaking? Really, what the heck is so important that Marisa and I meet? I mean, she's nuts, and I'm pathetic."

Arielle pauses and realizes this whole cause is being lost on Chris. "Let me back up and try to give you some context as to why this is important to the powers above. Do you believe there is a lot of good in this world and, by the same token, that there is a fair amount of evil roaming the world and that it takes all manner of shapes, sizes, and forms?"

"Okay, that's a reasonable statement," responds Chris.

"Believe it or not, there is a constant struggle between good and evil, every day, here, everywhere, and God in his wisdom 'elects' very specific individuals. More importantly, some individuals possess the capability to influence the cause of good in a very significant or popular way that will influence many others to follow their lead, resulting in the performance of more good deeds and behavior spreading exponentially. The net effect is that it serves the greater good of all humankind. These designated individuals have been identified because of their character, charisma, intelligence, personality, or some unique skill they possess or some combination of these qualities, but most importantly, because of their spirituality and love of God, either knowingly or subconsciously. Therefore, it is important to our cause that they succeed and reach their full potential for aiding our cause."

Chris acknowledges Arielle's explanation but challenges her one assumption.

"Since you know everything about me, you know I am no Holy Roller, and as a matter of fact, I have thought and said some very nasty things this last year about your boss after Theresa died."

"You see, Chris, it is exactly that honesty that is one of your redeeming qualities. But let me throw this back at you. Where did you go after our meeting that Sunday morning when you realized no one else saw us together, and you thought you were losing it?"

Chris sheepishly replies, "Okay, you got me on that."

"And how did you feel after spending some time in Church, Chris? Maybe a little more self-confident, a sense of inner peace that has been evading you for quite some time?"

Chris nods in agreement but then retorts, "If you know all this stuff is going to happen, then just give me the details of this strategy or plan and tell me what I need to do."

"Chris, you are smarter than that. You know it doesn't work that way. I was just a facilitator to get you to act a certain way. It was your choice to go to church that Sunday. Free will, Chris, free will. We can't make you do anything. We can only try to influence or nudge at times, depending on the situation. However, because of the relative importance of this spiritual endeavor, it was deemed significant enough that a direct intervention would be required. Hence, that is why we are spending all this quality time together." Arielle articulates with a sly grin.

Chris is absorbing all that he has heard with his eyes fixated on the graceful beauty that is standing in his den before him. Shaking his head in disbelief and with an air of skepticism, Chris is trying to rationalize in his mind everything that has taken place over these last few weeks, which has been now compounded by the fact that he is supposedly speaking with this angelic figure before him right in his den.

"I'm sorry, Arielle, but how am I supposed to believe any of this? First and foremost, that I am standing here, supposedly talking to an angel or a spiritual messenger. Second, that I need to hook up with this crazy lady that I barely know who has all this outrageous history and third, because of some future evil event, it is necessary that she and I join forces in some manner. How is any of this real? How am I supposed to believe any of this, and why should I? Why would any angelic figure visit or speak to me? None of this really makes any sense. And not for nothing. What the hell is with that freaking dog? Don't tell me Abbey is from some kind of pet heaven, or is she just some sort of heavenly prop?

Arielle, chuckling, understands Chris's cynicism. "Funny that you should bring up Abbey. The truth is, she is quite real."

"Abbey's real and she takes commands from an angelic spirit, who isn't real. Sure, that makes perfect sense," Chris responds now in utter frustration, along with every other rationalization Arielle has offered thus far.

"You've petted Abbey, and she's responded to you. Felt pretty real, right? Remember that first day, with her chasing the seagulls on the beach? She's been groomed to be a great service dog. All the more reason why I am now offering her to you as a gift of our friendship and, more importantly, I think somebody could use a loving companion."

"A dog, a dog is part of your big strategic plan? What am I going to do with a freaking dog? This is all too crazy. I need another drink."

"Take a second, Chris. Abbey, go to your new Master and give your paw to Chris." Abbey immediately crosses the floor and offers her paw to Chris and places it on his knee.

"Abbey will follow your every command and has been trained quite well. She is now all yours. Rather than grab that next drink, maybe you need to start working on forming new relationships. Granted, she's no Marisa, but you will find out she makes a great companion and will bring much joy and love into your life, so please accept this little gift on my behalf as a means of apologizing for deceiving you and meeting with you under false pretenses."

Chris stares at Abbey's captivating features, relents, and starts to stroke her beautiful coat. "A dog. She is a handsome-looking creature. I've always wanted one, but is she housebroken and trained to obey my orders? She doesn't know me."

"She knows you only too well. Go ahead, give her a command."

"Abbey, fetch my sweatshirt," Chris says as he points to a sweatshirt lying on the sofa. Abbey dashes over to the sofa and returns with his sweatshirt and places it on his lap, and then lies at his feet. "Good girl." Chris pats Abbey's head. "Okay, we got a deal, but can you explain to me, all this time you're floating all around or making all these plans with your boss, who's training this lovely creature? How can she even relate to you if you aren't real? You know, a human being?"

"Some things, Chris, are best left unexplained."

"Ha, now I got you," Chris eagerly exclaims.

"Chris, you are the one that is making all this so complicated. Remember, you don't have to believe anything that has occurred to date. You can brush off everything that has happened between you and me because no one else knows, nor would anyone ever believe you. As for Abbey, you can just say you found her as a stray on the beach and took her in since nobody ever claimed her. Marisa, you can just chalk that whole experience off as well. Anyone would totally understand. As I've told you, the choice is yours.

"You can go quietly about living your life in any way you choose. Every day in your life you make choices, some of little consequence and others of potentially great consequence. Yes, I am presenting a life-changing choice here. Should you decide to believe anything of what we've discussed, you can take up the gauntlet that lies before you and meet again with Marisa to see what happens. Or you can simply go about your life as if none of this happened and live it out as you see fit, escape all of it, and drink your way through life. However, before you make any final decisions let me try and give you some food for thought.

"How's your faith, Chris? Do you believe in a higher power, that you have a soul, that there is an afterlife? If the answer is yes, then as the Bible has shown us both in the old and new Testaments as well as in numerous subsequent accounts throughout history that there have been appearances of many angels taking a human form and appearing before specific people. Also, there have been numerous documented accounts in the Bible and throughout history up through the present day of angelic figures, visions, voices, and an infinite number of miracles that have interceded with everyday folks, not just great religious or historical figures. So, everything you are currently experiencing is, yes, extraordinary, but not out of the realms of possibility or being genuine.

"Before we take this next step, Chris, let me ask you again, do you believe? Is your faith strong? Do you believe in God? Do you accept those fundamental religious beliefs that you were taught and accepted without question during your youth?"

Chris is very solemn, pauses, and sighs. "Yes, even in my darkest moments, I guess I never truly stopped believing, and while my faith has certainly wavered, I've never lost faith in God and all that he or she represents."

"Okay, now let me offer one additional inducement to convince you that this is all quite believable and that what we are asking of you is very real. How's that shoulder, you know, the one that you had surgery on for a torn rotator cuff from your pitching days in college? No pain lately? You know how much that has pained you, off and on. Look at the scar on your shoulder."

Bewildered by her request, Chris goes to the nearest mirror in his den and pulls his shirt to the side, and the scar is gone. He stretches his arm out and even windmills his arm, with no pain; in fact, it feels stronger than it has in years.

Astonished at this latest experience, Chris stammers, "That's not possible. Why? Is this all you?"

"Let's remove any lingering doubts about who I am and why we are talking here. You see me quite clearly. You hear my words explicitly, and I have understood everything you have said to me, so now I ask you to take a little journey with me. Just look into my eyes." Chris hesitates and is somewhat unnerved by her request. "Come on, tough guy, you can do it. You want more proof. Here it is." Chris slowly approaches Arielle and sheepishly starts to focus his eyes on those glowing deep blue orbs of Arielle's.

Arielle moves closer, her eyes fixated on Chris as a glistening mist starts to envelop the growing luminous presence of Arielle. Their bodies never quite touch as Chris is now mesmerized by the enshrouding brilliant light within the mist that radiates from Arielle's presence. Immediately, he senses this warm glow fill his body as if the sun were shining brightly on his back, removing the chill of a winter's day, an inner warmth and feeling of lightness he has never experienced. They are swiftly transcended into a magnificent mystical alternate universe.

Chris is transfixed by the stunning, wondrous fast-moving scenes of majesty and splendor that pass before his eyes, like nothing he has ever experienced in this world. It was as if he had suddenly passed through some idyllic portal. A painted sky of such majesty and beauty bursting with a collage of enormous colorful clouds of indescribable splendor that flow and stretch forever, and a landscape filled with the greenest pastures and pastoral scenes that have ever befallen his eyesight. As he attempts to take it all in, he feels so small and insignificant surrounded by the size and scope of this magnificence. As one intense gorgeous scene passes another, he gains a whole new appreciation for the forces of nature and the grandeur of this alternate universe!

Suddenly, there is a dramatic change in the panoramic spectacle that he has been witnessing, and in an instant, a new vision appears, that of an emerald, green pasture that contains a figure of a small beautifully crafted bassinet that encompasses a small smiling baby swaddled in pastel blankets. With that, a sparkling misty veil enshrouds the baby, morphing into a toddler, small child, adolescent, young woman, older woman, then only an outline of the elderly woman, which transforms into hundreds of beautifully multi-colored butterflies that explode and vaporize into the sky. The process is repeated in rapid succession, faster and faster, as Chris slowly understands the communication being sent. That every human exists for a very small pocket of time in the overall passage of humanity's time on this planet, so yes, how does one make the best use of their limited time on this floating blue marble called earth? Does Chris want to make a difference and be a master of his fate or just be one of the infinite number of solitary individuals just drifting through the sea of life?

The vista of his portal rapidly changes again. This time, it is as if he has entered a utopian scene from Paradise with the most glorious flora and greenery filled with exquisite, majestic butterflies and heavenly birds. Off to the side he notices this lovely young woman standing beneath a magnificent tree as she now steps forward. Chris instantly recognizes the youthful beauty. It is Theresa. "Chris, follow me; I am the bridge for your new journey. This is the path to your future, your love, follow me. She turns and walks slowly along this scenic winding path."

"Theresa, wait, I have so much . . ." As Chris attempts to catch up to Theresa, however, no matter how fast he thinks he is moving, he consistently remains about fifty feet behind her.

Theresa stops and turns to face Chris and declares, "follow your new destiny," and with that she slowly morphs into the lovely, enchanting Marisa.

He is staggered by what he has just witnessed. Marisa states, "Join me, Chris. We have much to accomplish. With your love and passion, we can conquer any challenge, adversity or evil entity and build a life of happiness together forever." With that pronouncement, Marisa slowly fades into a pillowy white cloud, and the whole wondrous landscape changes one last time into an infinite incredulous ocean horizon as Chris senses he is now standing on an island shoreline with just the sound of the waves crashing on the sandy shore. He smells the aroma of the fresh sea and surrounding shore peppered with the sound of an occasional seagull passing by. He kneels, staring at the stunning ocean view and falls back in a sitting position, embracing the shoreline and feeling a deep sense of oneness, warmth, and serenity; he falls fast asleep.

Marisa and Chris

EARLY MORNING THE next day, Chris is awakened by the whimpering of a dog that badly needs to be taken out to relieve herself. Chris tries to gather his senses and, in a state of hazy consciousness, just stares at Abbey. Minutes pass as he tries to comprehend what he had experienced last night. Chris, desperately wanting a return to reality, focuses on Abbey. "I get it. Somebody needs to go out. Come on, let's take a walk while I try to clear my head." Chris lets Abbey take off outside as he follows along, trying to absorb what was real, and imagined and just how crazy his life has become. The cool morning sea air serves as a great tonic for awakening his intellect as he contemplates all that happened last evening and attempts to discern what was real and all that was discussed and witnessed. Abbey returns to Chris's side as he kneels to stroke her head and, looking into her eyes, starts chatting. "So, it is you and me, Abbey, against the world, huh? I guess I am supposed to believe everything that happened last night was the real deal because you are physically here and that, in some strange and fantastic way, my whole relationship with Arielle is real. Well, I'm going to need some time to figure this all out, but one thing I do know and that is both you and I could use some breakfast. So, let's see what, if anything, I have in the house will be good for you, otherwise I am going to have to do some shopping for my new best friend."

Chris spends the next few days setting up a dog-friendly home for Abbey, all the time holding random conversations with her as he mulls over the enormity of all that has transpired over these last few days. While he has been trying to sort out what decision path he will eventually take with his life and any next moves, he has come to the realization that in some spiritual or mystical way, Abbey is his connection to Arielle, or that is his emerging assumption. Why else would she leave this beautiful creature with Chris? Periodically, in some half-ass attempts, Chris will talk aloud to Abbey with the intent that it may send some signal to Arielle for her to reappear and provide some new or additional insight that will help him decide what path his future should take. However, no matter how loud, serious, funny, or sincere his entreaties to Abbey, they all go nowhere other than for her amusement and playfulness. Even though his pleas to Abbey are for naught, he still has the burning suspicion that there is some kind of connection between Abbey and Arielle, and he will get to the bottom of it. Right now, it looks like it is all up to him to make a decision and get on with his life.

After days of weighing all the pros and cons of his decision, in the final analysis, he can't help but come to the realization that what he has recently experienced is beyond any worldly experience. He fully grasped the message and their discussion as to whether he was going to be the master of his fate or just a passenger over the course of his journey through life. It has already changed his whole perspective on life from a driftwood existence to one of an invigorated fortune hunter ready to take on the new challenges that may lie ahead of him.

Moreover, there is still this unmistakable yearning for him to learn more about Marisa and that he is still attracted to her despite all that happened on their first date. Having decided to accept Arielle's inexplicable spiritual challenge, Chris must plan his next move on how to best connect to Marisa, because she is the key to all that the future holds for the both of them.

Chris ultimately decides that sometimes the best approach is being direct and decides to make plans to just meet at her address, which he obtained during his discussion with Detective Ramos. As the Detective had mentioned, Marisa was living for the time being with Rosita – the nurse from the hospital – in an apartment on the upper East Side. Having no way of knowing when she will be home, Chris decides to pick a late Sunday afternoon for his arrival at her apartment in the city. Having no luck after ringing the bell to her apartment, Chris decides to plant himself on one of the steps of the large porch leading up to the foyer of the two-story apartment building. Luckily it is a relatively sunny, mild October day as he waits, hopefully, to surprise Marisa and knows he will have to do some fast talking to make up for the way their last meeting ended.

After about a thirty-minute wait, he catches a glimpse of a familiar figure walking down the sidewalk headed in his direction. Sure enough, it is Marisa casually decked out in some sweats as she may have been running or doing some workout routine. Chris stands and steps down to the foot of the stairs, and with that, Marisa stops in her tracks. Quickly collecting her thoughts, she proceeds to her apartment and connects with her uninvited guest. "Somebody lose their directions to Central Park? But there is no running today because it is not pouring rain," Marisa blurts out sarcastically. "I guess chivalry and common civility are truly dead these days like so many people say."

Chris smiles sheepishly and says, "There is just no good way I can explain my horrible behavior during the storm that day," he hesitates. "Wait a second. Stay right here." He bolts about ten yards towards where his car is parked.

"Really? You're running away again? You have a hell of a way of impressing a girl."

Chris quickly returns with a beautiful bouquet of flowers. "I know this in no way makes up for any of my terrible behavior that day, but please accept this as the start of my apology."

Marisa quickly observes what is really a stunning arrangement of flowers and concurs, "Yes, this is a good start for a well-deserved apology."

Chris responds, "Here's the thing, that day at the park, you said some stuff that really blew me away, and I needed some time to think this through, and after some very heavy soul searching,

I think there is a lot of very stimulating information we need to share with one another."

Marisa smiles broadly. "Really? And I must confess and apologize for my part because, like you, I have given that day a lot of thought and realize that I should have handled that conversation a whole lot better."

Chris retorts, "Looks like we may be on the same page. So, how about we make a completely fresh start and be totally honest and open with one another, no matter how . . . uh . . . peculiar our revelations may become."

Hearing the breakthrough, she has desperately hoped for, Marisa is relieved beyond words and, now hiding her enthusiasm, responds, "You got yourself a deal, Chris."

They make plans to have dinner later that week, as both are very eager to hear in greater detail their individual stories, to say nothing that both of them have been yearning to spend some time together again. Chris selects one of his favorite haunts that has just the right romantic ambiance as well as providing them with a quiet location so they can start to share their respective stories. Marisa, looking as lovely as ever, finally gets her opportunity to explain in greater detail her remarkable saga. She describes in earnest everything surrounding her arrival on the Brooklyn shore as told to her by Detective Ramos, her otherworldly experience at the hospital, and the impact on her mindset, personality and how those mental images and memories of Theresa have haunted her. However, it was this overwhelming preoccupation with this woman, who goes by the name of Theresa, which enabled Marisa to make the Chris connection.

Chris, somewhat amazed by the astonishing information that Marisa has shared anew, is struck by the level of detail that Marisa is able to provide with respect to some of the events that took place during his relationship with Theresa. Chris responds in kind with an overview of his earlier years and then explains the nature of his whole relationship with Theresa and her death, but makes no mention of his relationship with, or appearances by, the mystical Arielle.

Both Marisa and Chris take some time to sit back and let their respective stories settle in, and now each of them has a much greater understanding of where they are each coming from and why their first date in Central Park became such an explosive event for the both of them.

Sharing these astounding details has undeniably brought them closer. Neither Chris nor Marisa gives in to their craving desire to be more intimate. However, Chris has one other burning question he needs to somehow phrase without him coming across as totally looney. That is, has she ever encountered Arielle, the true catalyst for everything that has happened to date? Chris, suppressing his true motive, tries to probe and asks during any of her bewildering transcendent mental experiences has she ever seen or stumbled upon any other mystifying individuals, but unfortunately, given her puzzled expression and response, she notes that there was not much more that she could handle. Even though Arielle had appeared at the hospital and was responsible for her revival, Marisa was just awakening from her coma as Arielle and Abbey spirited away. Chris brushes it off and changes subjects.

Following their long dinner and subsequent simmering feelings towards each other results in some heavy passionate embraces and kissing at the end of the evening. Chris is more convinced and committed than ever to going all in on Marisa and rolling the dice on their future together and accepting Arielle's challenge. With a sense of commitment and a renewed zest for the future of their relationship, Chris is truly excited about the prospect of building a relationship with Marisa, regardless whatever was in her past and the whole inexplicable Theresa factor. Their relationship takes off like a blazing comet, and Chris is clearly going to make up for whatever fate had robbed from him in his relationship with Theresa. Chris wined and dined Marisa as if she were a wondrous princess from a foreign land. Despite their past cultural differences, their love for one another grew stronger every day, as if they were always meant to be together.

For the next six months they traversed and romanced all over the world: Paris, the coast of Amalfi, Barcelona, Maui, Cabo, the Florida Keys and on and on. They were inseparable and were living a dream existence. One intriguing revelation that Chris was not prepared for was her faith. No matter what the location was, even on the most remote island, Marisa would seek out a church, as Rosita had certainly influenced her renewed interest in her faith. Regardless of the Church's religious affiliation, Marisa would seek out the nearest Church and make time to either attend the mass or, if none were available at the time, just go meditate or pray. Of course, she would drag Chris along and, out of the blue during one of their trips, ask him what he thought about "Divine intervention." Catching him by surprise, he asked her with respect to what, and she simply said, "Us. Do you think it was more than a random life coincidence that we ended up falling in love at this time in our lives, or was there some force or destiny pushing us to meet?"

Chris still refused at this point to even hint about his whole relationship with Arielle and her encouragement to meet again with Marisa, and just played dumb, knowing full well that her supposition about the influence of any "Divine intervention" was right on the money.

One of the more fascinating revelations for Chris was Marisa's athletic prowess. During their travels and overall time together, be it at a gym or some luxurious resort, Chris would kiddingly challenge Marisa to try some new adventure: hiking through difficult terrains and various water-based activities, and she either equaled or surpassed him in each of his boyish attempts to show off his own physical abilities Chris was amazed during her practice sessions in martial arts which she had been doing since she became a New Yorker. Chris would purposely go out of his way to find something he was either better at or that she had no clue about. Archery, shooting ranges, gym-based boot camp training. She either picked it up quickly or excelled at whatever he threw her way. She would simply say that it comes easy or that somewhere in her past she must have had some training in the specific skill they were playing around with that day. Chris, at times, would just shrug his shoulders and simply marvel at her skill set, all the while working his own ass off to keep up. Yet other times, he would muse to himself just who was this "Wonder Woman."

Moreover, Marisa is far from just being a one-dimensional woman; she has this insatiable thirst for knowledge of all things, but very specifically, Chris's business, as she has had no prior experience in the financial world. Her other unique qualities soon came to the fore, be it her obvious intelligence, ingratiating personality, or quick wit, all leading to a downright cocky kick-ass attitude that Chris finds stimulating and forces him to constantly elevate his own business game. Interspersed during their courtship and travels, Chris has been tutoring and providing business books, social media devices and even films such as Wall Street, The Big Short and The Wolf of Wall Street as some fodder for her to absorb and get a sense of his professional life.

Slowly Chris migrates her into his business relationships with his partners through dinners, informal business meetings and client schmooze fests. Whether some of it was learned from prior experiences from her past or from Theresa's memory vault, Marisa's business acumen grew swiftly from just being a voyeur of Chris's business life to an actual participant and outright asset contributing to the firm's growth and new successes. Once again, Chris is blindsided by Marisa's exceptional capabilities. What made this whole experience all the more exciting for Chris was watching her growth and transformation into a more and more confident businesswoman whose intelligence and athletic prowess were well beyond anything he had ever experienced with any other woman. Moreover, it was his hope that through all these new experiences, they would eventually bring her closer to unlocking the mystery of her true identity.

Intermingled with all these travels and business dealings, the personal and romantic relationship between them blossomed into the most passionate and loving experience Chris has ever known. Yes, he thought he would never love anyone like he did Theresa, but Marisa had taken them to a new level that Chris had never experienced with any woman. Whether it was her uninhibited nature, their undeniable chemistry, which led to unrequited passion and loving tender moments or just a melding of two remarkable personalities into a dynamic couple, there was no question that they were a perfect match. From Chris's perspective, he was a man reborn; Marisa had awakened his competitive juices not only from a business perspective but for life and all the challenges that may lie ahead, and he was ready to take them all on. However, for Marisa, there was one burning question that she always had on the tip of her tongue and finally, she broached the subject one lovely warm moonlit night in Cabo as they were walking off dinner on the beach.

"Chris, I need to ask you something that has always been bubbling around in my brain, not that it is any earth-shattering request, but I just need to know why you decided to see me again after that nightmare date, we had in Central Park."

Chris could sense that something along this line of questioning was bugging Marisa for some time
as their relationship bond and mutual thinking grew stronger. He also knew he was not about to reveal the unique and

mind-blowing experience he had with Arielle, whose prophecy was the catalyst for Chris seeking out Marisa again.

"I know what I am about to tell you is going to be out there somewhat, but you know how I have these vivid dreams be it about the past, work, whatever. Well, after our meeting in the park, some of those revelations you shared with me shook me up quite a bit. So, yes, you were constantly on my mind. Then one night, I had this remarkable dream. I was walking through some wooded area which was quite beautiful, when I heard or felt this angelic-like presence telling me to push forward as there was someone I needed to meet. I came to this stunning landscape with a small bridge hovering above a babbling stream. As I got to the middle of the bridge, I could see this image of a gorgeous woman standing on the other side. As I slowly moved closer, that woman was you. The voice whispered to me, 'Go to her. She will help you find your destiny.'" Chris thought to himself how deftly he had condensed his otherworld dream-like experience with Arielle.

"Are you telling me the absolute truth?"

"Marisa, I swear to God that happened; it is etched in my mind. There was no way I could not see you again. Hey, and not for nothing. What did I have to lose? I had no woman in my life. I was on the verge of becoming an alcoholic, and I had no interest in my business life anymore. I don't know if it was some quirk of fate, a spiritual push, or some other supernatural explanation, but that is what led me back to you. Not for nothing. Look where we are now, how happy and having the time of our lives, so there's no way I am going to question the wisdom of that dream or why it happened."

"Oh my God, Chris, don't you see, you are the key, the catalyst to unlocking my identity; it is just a matter of time. We are destined to take this life journey together and face all of life's challenges that lie ahead. I feel more empowered than ever."

Chris smiles. "Maybe, as you alluded to on the island, 'Divine intervention.'"

"Hey, you better not be making one of your bullcrap stories to appease me. I will throttle you."

"Okay, Okay, how about this?" Chris gives his half-ass imitation of Darth Vader's voice. "Marisa, I am your brother . . . father? Does that work for you?"

"You really can be a horse's ass when you work at it," Marisa responds. "So, tell me, oh Grand Wizard. What is our destiny? Where are we headed?"

Chris is now a little befuddled. "Are you talking about us or the future? Is this some inquisition as to what my intentions are for our relationship? Should I be shopping for some gaudy ring?"

"No, you ass." Marisa is now needling Chris. "As far as I am concerned, you proposed to me the day you returned and met me on the porch with those flowers. Don't you know we are already on our Honeymoon? What could possibly pass this experience." Slowly Marisa's mood turns serious and somewhat emotional as she grabs Chris by his arms and stares at him with those gorgeous berry brown eyes piercing his soul. "Chris, you are the love of my life. There was an immediate attraction between us from the first time we met at that Jersey shore party.

It was undeniable." As her eyes moisten, "I know you are my life partner, and I can't imagine any life without you. Call me crazy or obsessed, but I can't help it. I just am a different person when you are by my side."

Chris embraces Marisa in his arms. "Marisa, I love you more than life itself. You transformed my entire life. Before I met you, I was just a floating, no drowning man with no prospects or purpose in life. Your love has lifted my spirits to heights I never imagined possible. When I am with you, I feel as a couple, we are invincible and can conquer any potential hardship, challenge, or adversity that crosses our path. I just couldn't love anyone any more than I love you." As the tears run down Marisa's cheek, they embrace ever so lovingly and kiss with the warmest and deepest passion burning within their beating hearts.

Chris mused to himself, thinking again about Arielle as the two of them strode, holding hands under the warm, breezy moonlit night back to the hotel. Hovering on the shoreline in the background, a shimmering bright figure looks on and quietly says, "And so now they will face the greatest challenge of their lives, and the dark forces of evil will reveal themselves."

Marisa's Past Emerges

ON THEIR MOST current long weekend in Miami, as they were getting ready for dinner, Marisa was down at the bar overlooking the turquoise waters as Chris was stuck conducting some business on a phone conference in the hotel room. Relaxed, looking beautiful as ever sipping her martini, a swarthy gentleman sitting with a few associates noticed the exquisite Marisa at the bar and was suddenly stunned by her familiarity. The gentleman's curiosity overwhelming him, excused himself and headed towards Marisa at the bar. Standing a few feet away and ordering a drink, he glances over at Marisa and catches her eye.

"Excuse me for staring at such a beautiful lady, but you seem strangely familiar to me," states the man with a strong South American accent.

Marisa responds, "If that's your best line, I'm afraid that's not going to work for me, besides I am waiting for my boyfriend to join me."

"My apologies but have you ever lived or spent any time in Brazil, or do you happen to go by the name of Ana?"

"Sorry, pal, but that is strike two on Brazil and strike three on Ana."

With that, the gentleman headed to his room and not back to his table. In his room, the olive-skinned gentleman makes a quick phone call. "Is Baka there? This is Diego. I need to speak with him immediately."

After a few minutes go by, "Baka here. Is everything moving forward?"

Diego responds, "That is not why I am calling, but yes, everything is going well, but you will never believe the ghost I just spoke with. Moreover, she is the spitting image of your enduring nemesis and is very much alive and thriving."

"What are you talking about?" Baka says.

"Ana, Ana Moreno in the flesh."

"What? How is that possible? You must be mistaken," Baka responds incredulously.

"No, boss. From that dress she was wearing, I caught a partial glimpse of the infamous Moreno flaming Eagle tattoo and given her age, height and overall appearance, it looks like she is doing quite well."

"This is fucking unbelievable. They told me she drowned in that river. Carlos said he emptied his weapon when she hit the water. Send me some pictures, and I will know for sure, but use your fucking head and be very, very discreet and find anything else, everything you can. I need to know for sure. This is unfucking believable." Baka starts to rage over the phone. "Don't fuck this up. I must know, and as soon as possible."

Marisa is still at the bar as Chris arrives while several clandestine smartphone pictures are being taken by the gentleman from South America and sent directly to the individual, he just spoke with from his hotel room. Somewhere in the beautiful forests of Colombia, in a palatial estate, a man by the name of Baka is first startled and now fuming about this revelation as he screens the sequence of photos that have just been sent to him. He immediately calls one of his aides to find one of his henchmen; specifically, the one named Carlos, Baka explodes. Mystified as to why he has been suddenly summoned by his boss, Carlos enters the room, which was about to be filled with rage and outbursts of never-ending profanities from Baka.

"Tell me again how you erased the last remaining Moreno family member in NYC, specifically Ana. You do recall that little job I asked you to take care of?"

"Of course, boss, we pulled her off the street late in the night, brought her down to a deserted area by the East River and yeah, there was a scuffle as she managed to briefly break free with that little fucking knife she had hidden and wounded Manny. I slammed the back of her head with the butt of my gun, knocking her to the ground while I tended to Manny and yeah, she somehow managed to stagger up to her feet and then take off, but you know how good a shot I am, and even though she made it to that sewer-infested river, there is no way I missed as I emptied my gun. Manny will vouch for me. He was with me the whole time and has the wounds from her to prove it."

"Well, I guess her twin sister is alive and having a ball in Miami because I want you to look at these pictures and not for nothing. Check out that partial tat of what looks like a fucking flaming Eagle above her hip."

The back story here is that Baka, which roughly translates to demon in English, is one of the major and most ruthless Colombian successors to Pablo Escobar, and his main competitor at the time was the more benevolent and popular Moreno clan. As the competition had reached a fever pitch between the two emerging cartel families, Baka had had enough and took out the entire Moreno family and their loyal soldiers in a well-planned shocking, brutal attack on the Moreno estate via a car bombing in which all the Moreno family members and soldiers were eventually killed. However, as the smoke and confusion in an attack of this magnitude cleared, word came that one person had survived the well-planned multi-faceted attack, that being Ana, who was being groomed by her father Pablo to take over with her brother the Moreno business and fortunes. The day of the attack, Ana was supposed to be in the vehicle that had a planted ticking bomb attached, which killed her brother, but she was running late, and before she reached the vehicle, the bomb exploded as she was hit with some of the shrapnel, but her designated bodyguard Miguel swept her away from the battle riddled area as the main thrust of Baka's attack focused on the Moreno palatial estate.

For the next five years, Baka assumed control and more power in the drug trade emanating from Colombia and, thusly, emerged as Escobar's primary successor and dominant criminal force in all of Colombia. Baka, however, continued his search through various sources for the missing Moreno link as he knew only too well that Ana was extremely well-liked by the other Colombian families that possessed any wealth and power. So, it was of paramount importance to him that Ana be eliminated at all costs. Even though it was about three years later, during which time Ana had safely secured a new identity and life from a well-funded offshore account her father had set up for such an emergency and to find covert safety in the United States. Through his various nefarious connections, Baka eventually heard word that a woman resembling Ana was, in fact, alive and well in NYC. This then culminated in Baka sending two of his most trusted soldiers, Carlos, and Emanuel, to find and kill Ana once and for all.

"I don't normally believe in second chances," Baka states in slow and reserved anger, "but only because you have proved your worthiness and loyalty to me as you've handled all of your other assignments for me flawlessly, I will give you the opportunity to make this right. Only, this time, along with Manny, I want you to take two more of my most trusted soldiers, and when the job is completed, I want you to bring me the carve-out of her flesh with that fucking Eagle tattoo so that I know this time she is dead. To be honest, I would really like to have her detached head, but I don't want to cause any customs issues, so we'll keep it simple with the tattoo. And, one final word, if this gets fucked up in any way at all, don't bother coming back, and you better find a real new safe home for yourself." With a litany of profanities still ringing in his ears, Carlos, Manny and the two accompanying soldiers take off for the States.

Abbey has a Big Day

EVEN THOUGH THE relationship between Marisa and Chris was at a boiling point, and they discussed her moving in with him permanently, she still spent about fifty percent of her time living with Rosita in NYC. More to the point, she started attending part-time classes at Columbia, as well as working with Chris, wining and dining with new clients and working with his partners at his firm in Manhattan. So, it was not unusual for Marisa to be returning from one of her classes this early Spring Day and rushing up the stairs as she knew Chris was stopping by soon for them to meet some prospective new clients that evening. Unbeknownst to Marisa was a swarthy man not quite half a block away awaiting her return. Having staked out her apartment for the last few days, Carlos and Manny had hatched their plan to take care of Ana once and for all.

Carlos and Manny hopped out of their car about a block away once they got the "all clear" from their stake out partner. Carlos, Manny, and another of Baka's soldiers headed up the outside stairs to her apartment as Carlos reminded them about avoiding any gun play so as not to draw any attention to their malicious assignment. The fourth soldier was instructed to be the lookout, seated casually on her porch. Marisa and Rosita's apartment was on the second floor, and luckily for the encroaching threesome from Colombia, the first-floor apartment was vacant at this time, so any unusual noise above would go unnoticed, plus Rosita was out of town visiting some of her friends upstate. As they picked the lock on the main door to the entrance, they quietly made their way up the stairs to Marisa's apartment door. Not getting the usual buzz for company or delivery but a casual knock on the door, Marisa just assumed it was one of her more trusted neighbors who had key access to the main door downstairs and stopped by from time to time to chat. However, as soon as Marisa popped a crack in her door, it was slammed up on her as she went flying backwards, and the three hit men charged into her apartment.

Given her still ingrained amnesia state, Marisa did not recognize her previous assailants from well over a year ago, or their other associate. With a small revolver pointing at her face, Carlos orders Marisa to sit down on the kitchen chair as the other two search the remaining rooms in the apartment to make sure she is alone.

Marisa, still dealing with the shock of the bum rush at the door and racing heart, blurts out, "I have no idea why you are here, or you got the wrong apartment. Or if you are thinking of robbing me, you are going to be greatly disappointed."

At that, Carlos slaps Marisa across the face, and as she starts to jump out of the chair, Carlos orders Manny to tie her hands to the chair and shoves her back down. Marisa now fears a worst-case scenario as she senses something far more sinister is about to go down in her apartment. Rape or some kind of beating. What the hell was happening here?

As Carlos goes through her pocketbook and other personal items in the immediate area, "Marisa, is it now? Well, Ana, is your memory that short that you don't recognize your old friends Carlos and Manny from that night about a year ago down by the river? And yeah, Manny here has a very special score to settle with you. Where is that little knife of yours that you hide so well on your person?"

Unfortunately for Marisa, she is totally clueless as to what they are talking about, and she has no weapon of any kind on her. "I really think you have the wrong person. My name is not Ana, and I have no clue what you are talking about from a year ago."

With that, Carlos slaps her again on the face, drawing blood from her now swollen cheek and lip. Marisa's emotions are now hovering between terror and an emerging anger with that last blow to her face, but with that, Carlos turns to Manny and says, "Manny, I think you need to refresh Ana's memory, and maybe we should start to carve that little Eagle off her hip. Maybe that will wake her up and remind her of her roots." Carlos approaches with a rather large knife, but he says, "What is the hurry? Maybe we should have some fun with this beauty before we do all that carving, you know, in that back bedroom. I think Baka would like that. I know I would."

Pulling up in his car is Chris with the ever-present Abbey, as he always likes to take her for a run in the park nearby when he visits Marisa in the city. As Chris approaches, the guard on the porch, he quickly phones Carlos that Chris is approaching and asks if he should take any action.

"No, no, let him on in, and we will have a nice little party and take care of any possible loose ends. I want you to quietly follow him in and come up behind him when he gets ready to knock on her door." Chris sees the unfamiliar face on the porch and just nods as he bounds up the stairs with Abbey at his side and buzzes Marisa to let him on up. As Chris heads up the inside stairwell, he tells Abbey to wait at the top of the stairs as Rosita has allergy issues with dogs. Abbey sits atop the stairs as Chris approaches the door.

Inside the apartment, having untied Marisa, Manny is behind the door with that huge knife pointed at Marisa's side, and Carlos and the other soldier are on the other side of Marisa, out of eyesight. Luckily, under the guidance of Detective Ramos, he told Marisa to have a safe word with Chris whenever she was in imminent danger, given her suspect background issues. As soon as Chris starts his knock and Marisa starts to open the door, she shouts the safe word, and with that, Chris crashes through the open-door, slamming Manny to the floor and Marisa, free of any bonds, attacks Carlos and his companion as all hell breaks loose.

Simultaneously, the fourth fellow was quietly sneaking up the stairs when Chris exploded through the doorway. As he made his way up the stairs, Abbey's demeanor slowly changes from a curious look at the emerging stranger to a slow, low, growling anger as she senses her master's danger. The now somewhat startled stranger tries to calm the snarling, almost wolflike appearance of the German Shepherd that now lunges at the stranger, taking him down the stairs. Yelling a bunch of obscenities as the dog is all over him at the bottom of the stairs, he draws his large knife, and Abbey immediately reacts by attacking his wrist and part of the hand brandishing the knife. Using her powerful jaws, Abbey crunches and tears into the hand with her large teeth. Screaming and punching at Abbey, he tries to get his hand away from her locked jaw, dropping the knife and still punching away as Abbey is literally mangling his one hand. The stranger, with one powerful pull, rips his hand away, and with that there is a final crunch and snap. Screaming even more vigorously as Abbey has one of his fingers dangling from her mouth, blood spurting extensively from his hand, the man bursts out the main front door and down the porch sprinting recklessly down the street. Abbey temporarily parks herself, licking her wounds behind the main front door to ensure he doesn't return or pose any other potential threats to her master.

Meanwhile, there is an explosion of violence and ferocious brawling taking place inside Marisa's apartment. Marisa, using her martial arts skills, executes an excellent well-placed martial slam directly into Carlos's throat, immediately dropping him to his knees, gasping for air. The other soldier, despite Carlos's instructions, draws his weapon, and Marisa is now all over him as he is pulling it out. Concurrently, Chris and Manny are in a death match fighting over that huge knife of his after exchanging any number of blows, and Chris incurs one mean bloody slash on his arm. Finally, after an exhausting battle, Chris grabs an Iron lamp from a teetering table and smashes Manny's head, pretty much knocking him out. Using her martial arts talents to their full extent, Marisa has overpowered her adversary with several well-placed kicks to his stomach, face and, ultimately, his crotch, leaving him writhing in breathless pain on the floor.

However, before Marisa and Chris can turn their attention to Carlos, who has recovered sufficiently, he slams an unsuspecting Marisa's head against the brick section of the kitchen wall, knocking her out; now he has his weapon trained on Chris, who stops dead in his tracks. Carlos, regrouping from the blow to his throat and feeling more confident, checks on the one soldier still lying on the floor, but he is still in great pain and cursing out Marisa and yelling for Carlos to shoot her. Carefully, Carlos now takes his time checking out Manny, who is still out cold. Carlos starts to tell Chris he is first going to revive Marisa so Chris can watch as they rape and brutally murder her and then take their time finishing him off before they torch the whole building as they had originally planned.

However, the best plans often go awry, and Carlos is suddenly thrown against the wall as he is attacked by the bolting Abbey, who is all over him. During this time, Chris secures the gun from Carlos as he is still reeling from the sudden and intense attack from Abbey. Not taking any chances with Carlos, as he starts to pick himself up from the retreating Abbey, Chris, still holding the gun, picks up one of the broken leg chairs and lays Carlos out. With Manny and Carlos both unconscious and just the other adversary lying on the floor still in great pain, Chris ties him up with some curtain cords and immediately checks on Marisa and dials 911. During his emergency call, Chris asks the dispatcher on the line to see if she can put him through to Detective Ramos. Within a few minutes, Chris has Ramos on the line, and Ramos tells him to keep the line open and give him a quick briefing as to what happened while he grabs his team, immediately responding to the call.

Ramos arrives with his team and, while bolting halfway up the stairs, notices a bloody finger lying on the floor off to the side. "Is that a finger? Jesus Christ, what the hell happened here? Bag that."

He enters the chaotic scene that is Marisa's apartment. Chris is still unable to revive Marisa from her unconscious state; he explains to the EMTs what happened to her. Ramos has his men take Carlos, a now staggering Manny and the other soldier from Colombia into custody. As his men take the Colombian hitmen away, Detective Ramos stays with Chris and asks for as much detail as to what the hell happened and if he knew anything about who these guys were or why they launched such a vicious attack on Marisa.

Chris could offer no suggestions other than that they were there to rob and or rape Marisa. He asked if Ramos would take him to the hospital to be with Marisa while he continued to supply him with whatever other details he could offer about the whole nightmarish incident. While they were speeding to the hospital in Ramos's car, one thought quickly grabbed the Detective's attention.

He asks Chris, "Did you happen to notice whether all those combatants had all their fingers?"

Chris was very puzzled by the question. "As far as I know they all did, but I didn't have much time to take a physical inventory," he cryptically responded.

"No, the reason I ask is because there was a finger lying down on the floor by the entranceway, so maybe there was a fourth individual involved somehow."

Chris responds, "Wait a minute, there was this guy sitting on the porch when Abbey and I entered the building . . . maybe he was a lookout or something. If he was part of that gang, I bet Abbey took care of him. She's the real hero today, unbelievable, fighting off a possible fourth intruder and then rescuing all of us with that last-minute attack on the gunman."

Detective Ramos stops for a couple of seconds and says, "You mean to tell me your dog fought some other guy from getting to Marisa's apartment and then saved the day when she also attacked the guy holding the gun on you?"

"Yeah, she really is an exceptional creature, but honestly, I have never seen her get angry up until today when she lunged at the gunman with such ferocity."

"Wait, I have to get this out," as he reaches for his car radio. "We need an immediate notice to go to all the local hospitals and walk-in clinics to see if they have a nine-fingered patient with a badly bleeding hand." To Chris, "Remind me again where and when you adopted Ms. Abbey here?"

"I told you, Detective. I found her wandering the beach as a stray and took her in, and after sending out some notices, no one ever claimed her, so we've been best buds ever since."

Detective Ramos was now agitated. "I have way too much to unravel right now, but I will get to the bottom of this whole Abbey, the Wonder Dog issue. There's a lot more going on here."

The Emergence of Ana

WHEN CHRIS AND Detective Ramos arrive at the hospital, Marisa is already in a hospital bed hooked up to a variety of monitors and is still unconscious. In speaking with the attending physicians, they explain to both Chris and Ramos that, other than some bruises, she is fine. However, they have not been able to revive her and, given her prior history of head injuries, it is not surprising that she remains in this semi-coma state. They said at this time, it would be much better if she awakened from this condition on her own but under their watchful care. Chris settles in the hospital room, and Detective Ramos is anxious now to get to the Station house so he can start questioning the suspects that his team captured at the crime scene. Detective Ramos takes off, telling Chris if there is any change in her condition to contact him immediately on his cell phone.

As night falls in the hospital room, Chris, exhausted from the day's events, passes out while awaiting Marisa's recovery. During that night in the hospital room, Marisa's mind was flooded with all kinds of past and present images. In one dream sequence she meets what appears to be the image and spirit of Theresa, who has haunted her for so many months and informs Marisa that her work is done here, and she is moving on. Just like that, all memories, thoughts, and personality tics of Theresa are flushed from her mind and gone. As her mind in this subconscious state tries to fathom what has just happened, she finds herself in a new dream scenario, but one that is very familiar to her . . . her childhood, family, and an infinite number of memories of her past now flood her brain like a gushing waterfall. As the memories of her past pour in, filling her memory, the good and bad of her true identity; her monitors start moving erratically as with her rapid eye movements. Like water overflowing a riverbank, her brain reaches some kind of saturation point and moves her physically to a critical state of impending consciousness.

With the nurses and doctors rushing in and Chris by her side asking what is happening, she slowly regains consciousness and opens her eyes. As the haze of what her poor brain has just endured clears, she starts to gain some visual clarity. Tears running down her cheeks, she cries out for the one rock of stability in her life. "Chris? Chris?" He embraces her tenderly for a moment and is encouraged by the attending medical team to just wait outside while they conduct some cursory mental and physical tests on her overall condition. It is early morning, but

Chris calls Detective Ramos, who hops out of his bed and heads down to the hospital.

Once the doctors give Chris a very positive review of her overall condition, Chris and Marisa are left in the room to catch up. Chris immediately senses something has changed as he stares and observes the newfound excitement in her voice and movements

"Chris," she is almost shouting. "I know who I am. My name is Ana Moreno. I remember everything about me. There is no Marisa, no more Theresa. I am Ana Moreno from Colombia!!"

Chris, shocked by this revelation, is somewhat unnerved by what he just heard and is observing her slightly off demeanor.

"Oh my God, I know everything!" she says.

Chris, stammering sheepishly, asks, "Do you remember everything about us, our relationship?"

"Oh, YES, YES. I love you so much. Don't move or say a word. I have so much to tell you. Hold me, Chris. Hug me. I so love you. I just feel so alive!" With that, they embrace and kiss deeply and passionately.

Before she can share any more information with Chris, a ruffled Detective Ramos enters the room. "So, I see our little warrior has awakened from her slumber! She's good? No major issues?"

Chris responds, "Oh, she's more than good. Wait till you hear what she just told me." Ramos says, "Great, it seems we all have a lot of information to share, but our beautiful princess goes first."

Ramos says, "Great, it seems we all have a lot of information to share, but our beautiful princess goes first."

"Francisco, I know who I am. No more mystery. My name is Ana Moreno, and I grew up in Colombia and had to adopt a secret identity here in New York City because, as we all just found out, I have enemies that have sought me out from Colombia. They are members of the Baka cartel, no doubt."

The Detective listened attentively. "Okay, before I tell you what I found out last night during my interviews with your attackers, let me ask you one quick question. Are these the same guys that attacked you about a year ago and left you unconscious by the East River?"

"Yes. Well, two of them. Carlos and Manny first kidnapped and then attempted to kill me, but I managed to get away by jumping into the East River, which, luckily for me, was quite deep and the tide was moving rapidly in the same direction and helped carry me to safety as I could see some of his bullet's whiz by me in the water."

"Alright, we have a lot to discuss, but for now, I will give you the quick version, as we are still questioning these thugs and confirming some very dangerous assumptions. This is definitely a lot bigger than I ever imagined. Yes, the men who attacked you were Carlos, Emanuel, Jose, and Eduardo, all apparently soldiers from the Baka Cartel. Like I said, some information is still being confirmed by other DEA, ATF, and ICE sources.

"What I don't understand yet is why they have so far refused to give a motive for their attack. Right now, that is a big missing piece of the puzzle for me."

"I can fill that piece in for you," responds Ana. "I am the last remaining member of my family. Everyone else was murdered by the Baka Cartel when they launched their attack on my whole family and related soldiers. My bodyguard and monies made available to me through one of my father's discreet accounts made it possible for me to find a new life here in the United States. And what better place to hide than in plain sight in a city of eight million people that is filled with all kinds of nationalities?"

"Let me fully understand what you just revealed to us. You're saying that your family was also a cartel, I guess a rival cartel. And what was your role in this family business at that time?"

"I was simply the daughter of my father, Pablo Moreno and let me be clear, I had nothing to do with the business at that time. Was he grooming my brother and me to eventually take over his business? One could make that argument, but at the time of the attack and murder of my family, I had nothing to do with my father's business. My father, Pablo, was very deep in the drug business but was a very well-respected man in the Colombian Community and well-liked by all the other families except for the Baka clan, with whom we were bitter rivals, enemies I guess because both Cartels were becoming more and more wealthy and powerful in the Colombian arena."

Detective Ramos holds up his hand and says, "Okay, give me a minute here. This is a lot to take in. As a matter of fact, if you don't mind, Marisa, uh, sorry, Ana, you say is your real identity, this is all going to take some getting used to, and I would like to start recording your statements if you don't mind, so I don't miss or misconstrue any of what you are telling us."

With that comment, Chris responds, "I'm still reeling over here, fascinated and a bit freaked out, but, yeah, Ana, please tell us everything you can remember."

"No problem," Ana responds in what is now a slightly even heavier South American accent. "Let me take you back, if you don't mind, to my childhood because it is important that it will help you both better understand who I really am."

"Go for it," Ramos responds with his recorder all set up.

Ana begins, "We were always wealthy for as long as I can remember, and my father, Pablo, took great pains to give my brother and me the very best of everything, not in terms of spoiling us but by having us attend the best schools available. Additionally, and I'm sure at great expense, he made sure we also got the best physical training from various experts in their fields. He made sure we were taught English as well as our native tongue. In his own way, he was preparing us for any and all future challenges that may come our way, given the dangerous nature of his business. He basically trained my brother and me to be warriors in our own right when and if the time would ever come to utilize our skills. Of course, we played sports like soccer, tennis, etc., as well as training in archery, hand-to-hand combat, the use of any number of weapons, survival techniques . . . the whole gambit. However, given Pablo's personality, he taught us the importance of character, integrity, dignity, philanthropy and how fortunate we were and to help those who were less fortunate. Our mother died young of ovarian cancer, and over the years,

Pablo had other women around but none as a stepmother. He was the dominant parental figure in our lives."

There's a moment of silence, and Chris says, "Well, that sure explains a whole hell of a lot to me about who I have been sharing my life with and where all those hidden talents were developed."

Detective Ramos interrupts, "Let's fast forward to this whole Baka rivalry and the attack on your family."

Ana's somewhat upbeat tone now turns much more somber with a hint of subdued anger. "Well, once the whole void opened after Escobar's capture, there were years of chaos, in-fighting and all kinds of new corruption and the evolution of new cartel organizations. Long story short, the Baka and Moreno Cartel families managed to rise to the top with much bloodshed on both sides and to those that stood in their way. Make no mistake, my father, Pablo, could be as ruthless as he needed to be. Still, he was becoming more comfortable with his current station in life in terms of wealth and power. At the same time, the Baka clan wanted more and held no regard for any of the other smaller cartel families or the local inhabitants in general.

"Which leads us to the day of the attack. My brother and I had plans to attend a conference on developing greater infrastructure projects for Colombia. You know, better roads, a new bridge, that sort of thing which we were very involved with at the time. My brother was waiting for me along with his bodyguard in the car, and by some quirk of fate, I was delayed by one of my girlfriends who was informing me about her recent engagement. Before I could reach the car, along with my bodyguard, the car exploded. I was knocked down by the force of the blast and was hit with some shrapnel in my back. Stunned and bleeding badly at the time, my bodyguard whisked me away as we started to hear gunfire and all hell breaking loose at the main building of my father's estate. Bleeding and still foggy from the blast, I tried to take off to assist in the battle that was emerging at my father's estate, but unbeknownst to me, my bodyguard had strict instructions per my father's backup plan to get me out of the country should some attack of this magnitude ever take place. Hence, my long, sad journey to the States under the guidance and direction of my lifelong bodyguard, who was like an uncle to me as well as my protector."

Detective Ramos queries, "Where's this bodyguard or uncle now?"

"He died of a massive heart attack two years into our living in the States."

"Well, based on what you've told me so far, I don't see you being charged with any criminal activity, but you are going to have to explain everything all over again to the Feds, DEA in particular, as well as any other agency that has a need to know. Chris, get her the best lawyer you can that handles this type of situation because these Feds are really going to come at her.

"I still need to get what I can before the Feds take over this whole case, and there is only one really big issue, or should I say problem, for you right now, and that is you are still alive, and Baka is not going to be a happy camper once that news reaches him if it already has not."

With that, Ana speaks in a very firm and vengeful tone, "Well, fuck him and his whole fucking clan because now it is my turn, and I won't be waiting around for any of his thugs to find me."

"Whoa. Whoa. Let's all calm down a little. I know this has been a very rough journey for you but look at your life now with Chris and your future, besides once we get through this next ordeal with the Feds, let them do their thing with Baka, and we can take whatever needs to be done from there. I hate to say this, but more than likely, we will have to find you a safe house, and then the Feds are going to recommend the same thing only on their dime until they can bring Baka to justice."

"And hell will freeze over," responds a defiant Ana. "I have a world of revenge to take with my little buddy down south, and there is only one solution, and that is by taking him out and his whole fucking Cartel.

"Francisco, I know I owe you so much for what you did for me after that attack on the East River and gave me a whole new life that eventually brought me to Chris, but I must take control of my life now, and I am not going to any dance with the Feds or any other frigging federal agency. Chris and I are going to have some very heavy private discussions, and you are going to have to stall any Federal involvement for as long as you can so Chris and I can disappear for a while and figure out a new course of operation. Then and only then, we will loop you in if you want to play a very different role in this whole new evolving situation."

"Uh, Chris, do you have any idea of what she is talking about? Because I would love to hear what the hell is happening here."

"Detective, I think I am in the process of watching my life pass me by. I have no fucking clue what is bubbling in that brain of hers. This is all news to me."

"I am truly sorry, guys, but this is my time, and there is much to be accomplished." Ana's confidence and intentions appear to grow stronger by the minute.

"First things first. Let's get the hell out of this hospital. Francisco, I am begging you from the bottom of my heart, please do everything in your power to get me this delay with the Feds, and I promise Chris and I will reach out to you. You will have to make a very big decision at that time, but until then, please just let us take care of some very private business for now."

Ramos responds, "I know I am going to get a world of shit for this, but go ahead and make your plans, but as soon as the Feds get involved, we will need to find a new way to communicate because they are going to come after you with everything they got, and they have technologies I don't even know exist."

"Francisco, please come over here. I love you, and remember, I am still Marisa. Everything I just told you is for your eyes and ears only. Let them hear it eventually from Baka's hitmen, and you can be shocked when you hear the news, just like the Feds. I need to buy some time from any Federal interference as I already had some preliminary plans in the works on how to go after Baka before I was attacked and the whole amnesia episode. Tell the Feds when they unravel the story from those hitmen that Chris took me to Australia to go in hiding as protection from future attacks."

Detective Ramos responds, "That's a tall order, and I hope the Feds buy into that whole scenario, but I will stall them as much as possible from my end."

Ana then gives Ramos a huge hug. "I promise we will not let you down."

With that, Detective Ramos heads out the door to the station house. Ana then pulls Chris close to her and tells him, "Time is of the essence now, and we must move fast and furious. There is so very much that needs to be done."

"You will need to understand, Chris. Everything I am about to share with you was a plan that was being hatched by my bodyguard and me at the time, but we need to transition that plan into action now."

Much to the objection of the doctors, as they still wanted to run more tests, Ana secured her release from the hospital.

Ana Plans Her Revenge

CHRIS AND ANA head to his beach home down the Jersey Shore, as the NYC apartment is pretty much locked up by the police as a crime scene. On the car trip down to the Shore house, she shares more of what needs to be done to put her plan into action. She tells Chris she still has access to an enormous sum of money in that offshore account that is still unknown to the Feds, because once they find out about it, they will freeze and drain that account. Her plan, along with Chris's assistance, entails the contracting of mercenary soldiers, and that includes former Seal and other Special Forces operatives, all of whom are basically soldiers of fortune. The only two requirements are that they be loyal and discreet. Prior to her whole amnesia episode, she already had contact with a Black Ops contractor with whom her father had a prior relationship during her younger years of physical training under her father's guidance.

Additionally, she had been in constant contact with one of her cousins (Marco) who was working with the other smaller cartel families in Colombia. Ana was building an army of combined mercenary soldiers and volunteer soldiers from the other Colombian families, all of whom have been scarred or fed up with Baka's ruthless handling of local affairs and the political corruption that was being controlled by Baka's police puppets. The mercenary soldiers would be the tip of the sword, backed up by the combined family's warriors. Ana was clear in her commitment to this plan with Chris; she would be going forward with him or without him, as she needed to avenge her family's murder. Moreover, she needed to be on the offensive now, as Baka was fully aware of her existence and whereabouts. Chris reminded Ana about their conversation in Cabo that romantic evening and how together they are invincible, so their fate and destiny are forever interwoven, and there is no way he would ever let her go it alone.

Ana needed now to explain in more detail her past and relationship with her father and brother. Ana began, "You already know how my father was grooming Miguel and me to eventually take over the business. Pablo has reached some very key decisions as to our roles going forward. Based on what he saw during our education and physical training by former Special Forces soldiers, he reached some very salient conclusions, considering our personal proclivities as well. He felt Miguel would be the one to take over the reins of the business, and I would be more behind the scenes as his protector and or enforcer when it would be deemed necessary.

"This was all based on the feedback as well as his own observations on our performance during our training. It became clear as time progressed that Miguel was the businessman and had good physical talents, but mine were far superior, and the trainers kiddingly gave me the nickname of 'warrior princess,' which kind of stuck as well as got around not only our estate but seeped into the community at different events that we all participated. Now you can understand and see who I truly am now that I have recovered fully from my amnesia episodes. I am that warrior princess. This is what I was trained for, and Baka and his followers will feel the full wrath of my prowess."

Chris responded, "I totally understand and very much appreciate you filling in a lot of blanks for me, but you'll have to understand this is also a big adjustment for me as I embrace this new dimension and personality of Ana. Can I ask, are there any secret superpowers I should know about before we proceed any further?"

Laughing, Ana responds, "I guess that is why I love you so much, because you can be such an ass at times and keep me grounded."

"Hey, invincible partners. That's us," Chris retorts, "and not for nothing. I wouldn't be surprised you have some hidden guardians you are not even aware of." The first time Chris alludes to Arielle's role, Ana just shoots him a bewildered expression but has too much on her mind to pursue what she feels is Chris's continued teasing.

Ana shares one more revealing component of her father's story, which had to do with his future plans for his children and business. "You must understand more as to who my father was and his plans for his business as well as for Miguel and me. He was in the process of exploring his options for transitioning out of the drug business, which may be one of the reasons Baka moved on him when he did, because he was aware of Pablo's future intentions. Pablo wanted very much to turn away from his past and transition his whole business empire into growing tobacco and sugar cane so that Miguel and I would not have to deal with the inevitable skirmishes or battles with Baka and any other ambitious cartels. Moreover, he wanted to spare us from any legal issues we would have to deal with from various authorities.

"Miguel, as I mentioned, would handle all the business and legal-related issues to transform Pablo's empire under his guidance, and I would work with the agricultural specialists in the fields as well as be the face of his new business and philanthropic efforts for the surrounding community. He wanted to establish some specific charitable organizations to help the various families that were struggling financially or with healthcare issues, as well as join some of the national charities and attempt to change in some small way his whole social profile.

"How could I not adore the most important male figure in my life and rejoice in his altruistic ambitions to change his entire way of life for the good of all? That is why his and Miguel's deaths and how they both died have burned like volcanic embers in my soul. I could never be at peace in my heart until this revenge was extracted. I just hope that all that I have shared with you gives you some perspective as to why I am on this dark mission of vengeance."

Chris responds with a weak smile, "I guess deep down I knew our fun ride would end soon, just not so violently and abruptly, but I love you more than life itself, and together we make one hell of an unbeatable team."

They embrace in a long, deep passionate kiss, Ana with her eyes tearing up. "I love you more than ever," she said.

Back to business and Ana's plan. Ana and Chris needed to establish a base of operations close to Colombia, yet far enough away to avoid suspicions. Ana selected Gorgona Island, which is about 28km from Colombia. Ana re-established communications with her cousin Marco in South America and got an update as to what had transpired during the break in their communications. Much had changed as Baka was exercising greater control and power over the surrounding Colombian community since he had the deputy mayor in his pocket as well as the Chief of Police and his lieutenants. Baka had initiated his own reign of terror once he had vanquished all opposition. In addition to the expansion of his drug empire and political corruption, he managed a huge prostitution and female trafficking ring by literally stealing beautiful young girls from the community families either by forcing them into drug dependence or via other twisted means. His evil shadow cast a pall of darkness over the entire community. The devil himself couldn't have appointed a better caretaker for all these pernicious activities managed by Baka and his lieutenants.

All this news fell hard on Ana's heart, and she was more motivated than ever to move swiftly with her plans to eradicate Baka's malevolent circus. Chris, working closely with Ana, is in heavy negotiations with the Black Ops company, not only to secure a significant number of soldiers with various lethal skill sets but also to rent some heavy artillery. During their negotiations with the Black Ops executive, Ana asks about the availability of some top-of-the-line helicopters.

Chris pulls Ana aside. "Do you really have that kind of money, and just how massive is this military initiative?"

Ana explains that she will need that kind of firepower to soften up and destroy Baka's compound as he had built it up over the years like a fortress that would warrant that kind of firepower. Chris backs off, and Ana secures a Bell Viper chopper, which is an update to the Cobra and has the most advanced weaponry equipment. Moreover, it is the only chopper that has air-to-missile capability. She additionally wants a fighter chopper by renting the use of the 64 D Apache, which is among the best combat copters. She gets assurance that she will have a top-notch crew to man each machine for the attack on Baka's estate.

Her plan is to have the choppers level as much of his estate and destroy his accompanying opium fields and production factory, Then have the combined families led by Marco and his soldiers launch their attack on the palace wreckage and surviving forces at the Baka fortress. That is one major objective of her plan, and the other is to have Baka and whatever soldiers he takes with him meet one on one in a separate location to take on Ana and her soldiers in a separate battle to the death. With

Marco's assistance, Ana found a strategic locale. It's a small, relatively deserted old Church mission with some surrounding monastic buildings that she would use as her base for meeting Baka head-on, which was about a good ten miles away from his palatial fortress. In essence, this must be a perfectly timed two-prong attack during which Ana will have some team members with the capability to jam all of Baka's communications, so he has no idea that his estate is under attack while he is conducting his personal battle with Ana and her troops.

Ana and Chris leave for Gorgona Island. As promised, it is now time for her to reach out to her old compadre, Detective Ramos. In a very lengthy call, she gives the Detective an overview of what her plan is. Realizing the life-threatening commitment, she is asking as to whether he wants to join them in Colombia. The one guarantee she offers is if all goes well, he will never have to work again as she will set him up for life financially or if things go south to his designated heirs. Detective Ramos is blown away by the magnitude of what he would be part of as well as the potential reward; and asks for twenty-four hours to think about this life-changing event. After some very thoughtful consideration, Francisco decides to stay in his current role as he explains he can keep tabs on whatever federal information he is privy to or snoops out about her case and their ongoing search for Ana. Additionally, he can try and provide false leads and keep her covert activities just that until everything explodes. Ana appreciates his role and agrees that it is a much greater use of his resources and there will still be a huge financial benefit for him when the dust eventually clears. They make plans for a continued covert line of communication.

"Oh, one other favor, Francisco, and this request is from Chris."

Chris jumps on the phone now. "I have a big ask, but it, hopefully, is only temporary and because I know you have a special interest in what I am about to ask."

Frank responds with an air of curiosity, "Sure, whatever you need, Chris."

"Would you mind taking care of Abbey for the interim? Maybe in some way, over time, she will help you fill in some of the blanks to the questions you have about her past," Chris jokingly requests. "Seriously, Frank. Abbey is an incredible sweetheart of a dog, but you may be able to utilize some of her skills, which, as you will learn over time, are abundant, and maybe you can even use some of her talents in any future cases. She is a canine without a peer."

"Chris, I would be delighted, and it will give me the opportunity to check out her past, more importantly, where she really came from through some colleague connections I have in the canine industry. Worse case, I could certainly use the companionship, as I know I will take a lot of ribbing at the station house once they hear about my new 'girlfriend.'"

"Frank, I can't thank you enough and believe me, once you bond with her, you will have a compadre for life."

"God speed, Chris and take care of 'our girl' for me. You know she means a lot more than any case I have ever worked."

"You got it, Frank, and thanks for keeping the Feds off our backs for as long as you can."

On the island of Gorgona, Ana and Chris hold their first strategic meeting with the leader of the Black Ops team, the copter team and Marco. The first briefing gives a high-level overview of the plan and any potential shortcomings that any of the participants foresee. Over the next few days, the core leaders from each team hash out the details and timing of all that needs to take place in the following days. Roles are defined, specific tactics discussed, the need to disrupt the communications capability within the Baka teams is detailed, and plans for a first strike at the political arm of Baka's operation are drawn up, all under Ana's direction. The leaders of the Black Ops team make it clear to Ana and Chris that this will have to be very much a guerilla-type of encounter since the landscape is jungle based – meaning they will have to move about in small teams, use much camouflage and integrate the use of IED landmines where they can expect the opposition to take up positions. At times there will be some very close-up combat situations, again because of the surrounding thick jungle. During their whole time in this planning stage, Ana and Chris have been getting a special crash course in combat and physical training from the Black Ops team, so they are as combat-ready as possible, given this short time span.

Based on Marco's research and reports from other neighbors familiar with the Baka families' activities, they typically take their teenage children to their various sporting events every Saturday. There is a big local soccer tournament five miles from home this Saturday. Then usually the mother, along with the kids and a few relatives, go shopping near Bogota and eat at their favorite restaurant. It was decided that this upcoming Saturday would serve as D-day for their planned attack. Concurrent to all these activities, Ana has cut her hair and looking at her during their training sessions Chris can't help but notice that more than ever in her combat fatigues and new hairdo Ana, looks more than ever like the "warrior princess" he has heard so much about.

More importantly, Ana needs to enact her plan to get Baka to meet her at the deserted Church location. Ana decides to take the direct approach and, through a burner phone, contacts Baka directly and informs him she is on her way to Colombia as his two attacks on her life have clearly shaken her, and she wants to make a deal and get some assurances for her safety. She informs him that she wants to meet him face-to-face to discuss an alternative peace plan between the two families. Her offer is to promise never to take any future actions against Baka and or his family in exchange for her own protection, as she would be willing to move back to the area and basically live a life in isolation away from him. She would never form any army or take any individual actions against him or his family in exchange for her freedom to just live her life out in peace back in her homeland, as she can no longer deal with living in fear of his attacks while she resides in the U.S. She leaves this as a message on his phone in the middle of the night and awaits his response via email to a temporary email address set up by her military communications specialist.

The date of the meeting, location of the Church site and time were all provided. For her own protection, she also detailed that she would not be alone and have adequate personnel protection for the meeting. Knowing full well that Baka will come prepared with a cadre of soldiers, if not a small army, because he will have no intention of negotiating any kind of peace considering Ana's inferior position militarily. Baka will see this as his golden opportunity to eliminate Ana and any influence she may still have on the community. Ana is clearly counting on Baka's huge ego and thirst for power to underestimate any bellicose action she may have planned for him. The whole key to their plan is to have Baka far away from his compound so they can launch their more massive and destructive mission against his home-based forces and fortress. The call had been made that night, and sure enough, around noon the next day, Baka agreed to the date, time, and location for their meeting. The trap is set.

Next, however, before any significant military move can be made, Ana needs to eliminate Baka's political influence as much as she can by taking out some key personnel, again, based on Marco's information. He explains how the Deputy Mayor has a 'special relationship' with a woman who is not his wife whom he meets every Friday night in a remote rural area under the guise of a card game with his buddies and typically leaves in the early morning to head back home. Plans are drawn up to have a Special Forces sniper take him out first thing that Saturday morning. When word spreads to the police department, the waiting sniper will hit the police Chief's car, hopefully including his close lieutenants' car also, with a grenade launcher and blow the cars to smithereens, thereby eliminating any potential assistance from any police forces as they will all be running around trying to find out who was behind these startling and abrupt assassinations.

The Angel of Death Arrives

THAT SATURDAY MORNING arrives crisp, mild, and sunny. It is like every morning in the small bucolic village except for one oddity. Perched on a bluff above the town, hidden by a small cluster of shrubs, a scoped rifle barrel is stalking its prey. Like clockwork, the Deputy Mayor shuts the door to his paramour's home and heads to his car about fifty yards down the small village block. A short pop crackles through the morning air, and the Deputy Mayor crumples in place as if his body is balloon-like and is punctured with a gaping hole. As there are only a handful of villagers within sight of the Deputy Mayor's body, they are startled at the man now lying on the ground bleeding and motionless. As they rush over in his direction, the ominous flow of blood steadily increases. Instead of checking on someone they thought may have just passed out, there is a cry for help, and calls are made to emergency services and to the police.

Roughly about thirty minutes later, because of its location from the police station, two police cars arrive, and as the local townspeople start to clear the area for the arriving cars, a rapid swoosh cuts through the air, and a huge explosion destroys the first police vehicle immediately followed by a second explosive burst that destroys the other police car and all its occupants. All the previously gathered inhabitants now seek refuge, and the small village is completely shut down in paralysis for fear of any additional attacks. Meanwhile, the sniper stealthily makes his way down the bluff, slipping away from his previous high vantage point, walking calmly to his vehicle, and heading to Ana's location, notifying her that mission one is accomplished.

Baka is preparing to meet his nemesis at the appointed Church location at 1:00 pm and has laid out his own plan of attack on Ana and any accompanying comrades. He makes it very clear that all enemy combatants must be killed except Ana; she must be saved at all costs for him to personally address her mode of death. When news of the Deputy Mayor's assassination and the explosive nature of the Police Chief and his Lieutenants' demise reaches Baka, he clearly knows who was behind such an egregious attack and calls for more of his soldiers to accompany him on his trip to meet Ana. His anger and suspicions about this event increase his resolve to eviscerate Ana once and for all. Baka leads his small army on their journey to meet up with Ana and is prepared to address whatever new tricks she may have planned. However, unbeknownst to Baka, there are two heavily laden weaponized choppers in transit to his compound-estate location. Additionally, about a mile away from his palace in a deep woodland location, a small army has formed and is making its way to move on Baka's estate once the choppers have wreaked their devastation on his palatial estate, his drug-producing factory and opium fields.

Ana is finalizing all the strategic and tactical placements of her Special Ops soldiers in and around the church complex and has received the green light from her communications team that they are finalizing the disruption of Baka's communications capability. After Ana has her brief face-to-face encounter with Baka and his lieutenants, she and Chris will swiftly retreat towards the Church building and escape into the jungle area to lead the awaiting Black Ops team through the thick jungle from the right flank, while the snipers try to pick off any of Baka's men controlling the potential heavy weaponry his soldiers will be using. Additionally, the other Black Ops teams will be moving from the left flank via the jungle in a pincer-like operation to wipe out Baka's forces.

While Ana and Chris await Baka's arrival, Chris wants to share some final thoughts with Ana, given the dire circumstances they are about to encounter. Chris says, "Regardless of how this whole enterprise turns out, remember my love for you is infinite, and I will follow you to the depths of hell."

Ana responds, "Boy, how about a little more faith in the outcome? I have every intention of winning this battle and the total destruction of his drug and criminal empire. I know I have been a bear with respect to my intensity and vengeful attitude, but this is truly a battle of good versus evil. Moreover, I am not going to let anything happen to you. Give me some credit. We've really planned this whole operation out. Where's your faith?"

Chris pauses a moment and is thunderstruck by his surprising realization. "Faith, your faith. That has always been your essence, and that is your secret power. The whole Divine intervention theme you've been espousing for so long. I am so glad you asked about faith and this whole good versus evil scenario because there is something I need to tell you that supports your Divine intervention scenario. I better say something now before all hell breaks loose. I want to give you this one, but very important piece of advice should you, by some small chance, find yourself in a desperate and hopeless situation. There is a very special person I would like you to reach out to, and this person is more powerful than any earthly army or any human that I know of. Her name is Arielle."

Ana is totally baffled by Chris's revelation. "What in God's name are you talking about?"

Chris responds, "Exactly, that is what I am talking about. You have, let's say, a secret admirer," Chris smiles, "no, really a protector who will be there for you. Just call her name, and after this whole fiasco is over, I will tell you everything, but I am dead serious here. Promise me, worst-case scenario, call out to her. You have friends in some very high places."

Ana is still quite mystified by Chris's very strange request, but there is no time now as Baka and his team of soldiers arrive in a row of jeeps and other military vehicles. While all of Ana's mercenaries are already in their tactical positions, she walks out in front of the Church along with Chris at her side and two of her lead soldiers flanking her position. Baka, in the lead jeep, stops his small envoy about twenty yards from Ana's position and walks up to meet her, flanked by a handful of his mercenaries. Walking slowly, surveying the landscape for any hint as to where her troops may be positioned, Baka instructs his team leads to move into their positions while he speaks with Ana.

Now about five feet away, Baka speaks, "So it really is true. You are here in the flesh, very bold move or incredibly reckless and foolish. Did you honestly intend to negotiate some kind of arrangement between the two of us?"

Ana responds, "The only real negotiations between you and me, Baka, is who will surrender first."

Baka starts laughing. "Well, then, this will be a very short conversation and visit because you might as well surrender right now, as you are clearly outnumbered."

Again, Ana responds, "Do you really think I would show all my cards for you to see? You will soon find out just how well-placed my troops are."

With that, Baka then raises his one arm as some sort of signal, and with that, another military truck comes rumbling out of hiding, and a whole other platoon of soldiers unloads from the truck. "How do you feel about your odds of walking out of here victorious now, Ana? Even for the so-called great 'warrior princess,'" he mockingly retorts, "how could you even think of trying to take me on at the height of my power and influence? You are not in the U.S. any longer. You are on my turf, my land. This is my kingdom that you dared to enter and will suffer unbearable consequences. I only feel bad for all these poor soldiers that are going to die for a useless cause for them because this is only a personal blood feud just between you and me."

It is now Ana's turn to chuckle a little. "Well, you got the personal bitter blood feud part right, but you grossly underestimated the grand scope and nature of this meeting today. I've been planning for this day since you brutally murdered my father and brother; do you think I would just undertake a plan to meet you and your small army head-on? No, this is a battle of good versus evil for the soul of this land and to save thousands of future lives. Your evil reign is going to end today. All the suffering, torture, trafficking, and drug-fueled hysteria you have supervised for years is going up in flames like the hell you came from. You are the personification of all that is evil in this land. I am staring at 'El Diablo' in person. You mockingly referred to me as the 'warrior princess,' maybe you should be thinking about me as 'the Angel of Death,' yours in particular."

Nobody has ever spoken to Baka in such an abrasive and condescending tone, and clearly his demeanor now is turning to his true colors. He starts to reply, but Ana interrupts him. "Baka, who do you think had those political hacks of yours killed today, and as we stand here, who do you think has launched a savage all-out attack on your palatial fortress?"

Baka erupts. "Who the fuck do you think you are talking to? Where would you ever get the balls or resources to launch any kind of attack? The people in the village by my estate live in fear of my very shadow; they are nothing but farmers and small-time merchants. Where are you getting the military might and forces to take on my fortress?"

Ana replies, "People that reach your height of power and money think they are beyond reproach and are untouchable. Their ego and narcissistic ways cloud their thinking. That is why it was so easy for me to pull you and some of your top soldiers away from your estate, because your hate and feeling of invincibility to meet me head-on overwhelmed any concern for your home base."

Baka orders his top lieutenant to contact his lead soldiers at his compound, but all they get is static. He tries his phone and orders those around him to contact their counterparts at his estate, but to no avail.

"Problem with your communications, Baka?" Ana asks derisively.

Baka shouts, "What the hell is going on here? Nobody can tell me what is happening at my compound . . ."

Ana interrupts, "Even if they could, you wouldn't be able to speak with many of your soldiers as they are under heavy attack."

"I don't believe you. That's impossible. No one has the military resources or forces to take me on."

"Believe what you want, Baka, but your empire is crumbling as we speak."

With that, he dispatches two soldiers to head back immediately to his estate and report back to him what, if anything, is going on back home.

Baka is furious and doing everything he can to control his rage and just blow Ana away right now. He manages to regain control of his emotions. "Okay, you have had your fun. Now it is my turn." Baka continues, "I will not only make sure any and every soldier that chose to fight alongside you today will be dead before the sun sets, but for you I have a special treat, a very slow and painful death in which I will personally remove one ear, one eye, your nose and then set fire to your body, and the final blow will be your beheading while your flesh is melting away. I have already instructed my soldiers that nobody must harm you. You will be the last person standing, and then I will finally get the thrill of ending your life that I have longed for all these years."

Chris finds his opening. "Well, this has really been fun with everybody getting reacquainted. Why don't we end all this 'getting to know you again' talk and get down to business?"

"Wait a minute," Baka responds. "Is this the so-called boyfriend, the lover I have heard about from the States?"

"Yep, the one and only."

"Well then, let me revise my instructions to my troops. Take a good look. I want this one alive with Ana, so I can personally supervise his death in front of Ana just for some added spice. Oh, thank you, amigo, for adding to my fun."

"Hey, no problem, big daddy, but really we need to get down to the real reason why we are all here." With that, Chris signals to his soldiers with a specific hand gesture as Ana, Chris and the flanking soldiers start their retreat towards the Church.

There is a ferocious burst of bullets and mini explosions from all sides. A small cadre of Baka's soldiers is immediately wiped out by Ana's well-placed snipers. Chris and Ana retreat swiftly towards the Church as planned, but covertly move deep into the jungle to meet up with the Black Ops and head up their movement on Baka's troops. Both sides are using a variety of machine guns, grenade launching and assorted automatic rifle fire, with Baka's team having the advantage of using handheld missile weapons, which at the current time were exploding massive holes into the church structure with concrete boulders flying in every direction. Ana had strategically placed three snipers in elevated triangular positions so they would have the advantage of picking Baka's soldiers off, especially those using any of the heavy weapons – handheld missiles, grenade launchers, etc. – until their location was finally discovered.

Ana had her team of mercenaries' place weapons in and around the Church openings and fissure-like holes as if they were all positioned in the Church. In reality, as they all ran towards the Church, Chris and Ana covertly moved into the heavily wooded area because they knew Baka would focus his initial attack on the Church and level it with his missile and grenade launchers. While all the Special Ops soldiers on Ana's team were well placed in heavily wooded forest areas and in and around lofty rock formations for protection, Chris and Ana would constantly be moving through the jungle along with the Black Ops team working the best vantage points to attack Baka's troops. The one grave mistake Ana made in her planning was that she underestimated the number of soldiers Baka would bring with him to the battle. He wanted to make sure there was no way Ana would escape his grasp this time, and he came to battle more than prepared, easily outnumbering her troops overwhelmingly.

Meanwhile, back at Baka's estate, the two military choppers had swooped in without any warning and, facing no counterfire at first, hit Baka's barracks, which housed the bulk of his remaining troops that he didn't take with him. The choppers leveled all the primary structures within the grounds of the estate as well as any standing military weapons. Now their focus shifted to the outer structure of the fortress, taking out huge concrete fragments. That coupled with the relentless machine gun attack from the Apache helicopter, Baka's soldiers were being annihilated. Any time Baka's soldiers found a new protected defensive position to fire back at the choppers, a missile would soon find its target, demolishing the structure and obliterating the soldiers. Once the choppers had completed their initial mission of destroying Baka's fortress, they moved on to his drug factory and opium fields. The army of Colombian countrymen led by Marco launched their attack on any remaining troops or resistance at the fortress. Marco's army moved forward, taking on only small pockets of resistance. Ana's plan was flawless. The beating heart of Baka's empire was all but dead, as the choppers were now in the process of setting fire to his various localized opium fields and drug-producing factories.

True to form, Baka focused his attack on the Church, blowing enormous holes into the concrete structure and generating vast chunks of falling concrete and debris, hopefully crushing any enemy combatants who remained in the building. However, whenever any small groups of Baka's soldiers would initiate any movement towards the Church, they would encounter, much to their surprise and misfortune, strategically placed IED landmines, resulting in numerous casualties. As each side was able to penetrate key defensive positions, gaining individual and minor victories, the body counts on both sides were mounting rapidly. The savagery and intense nature of the battle waged for well over four hours; however, as the number of casualties mounted on each side, the overwhelming pounding of gunfire and explosions diminished proportionately. Sadly, most of the gunfire and troop movements were coming from Baka's side, as there was only a smattering of return fire from Ana, Chris, and the few remaining soldiers. During one fierce exchange between Ana, Chris and Baka's troops, Chris took a bullet in the left shoulder and was already dealing with a bad leg that had taken on some shrapnel from a grenade when he threw his body over Ana's, protecting her from the blast.

During the tactical planning stage, Ana informed the mercenary soldiers if any of them felt that a defeat was imminent, they were free to make their way back to Baka's estate and join up with Marco's army. This was never meant to be a suicide mission for them. Ana and Chris eventually worked their way back to the shredded remains of the Church structure for cover and took some time to assess their situation at this point. Baka, already sensing victory, ordered a significant number of his troops to collect their casualties and head back to his estate, as he was clearly worried that he had never received any word from the two soldiers he dispatched to his estate earlier. Ana was on the brink of tears and despair, not only because of their current circumstances but for all the lost professional soldiers that supported her cause, even though they fully understood the severity of the risk involved in undertaking such an assignment.

Ana girds her emotions and speaks, "They still have that one fucking mounted machine gun which has been hammering us in addition to the fact that they clearly outnumber us, and I can't raise any communications from any of our remaining comrades; they have either taken off or are just too badly injured to fight anymore."

Chris, trying to manage his injuries without making Ana feel any worse about their overall situation, tries to lighten the mood. "Hey, Ana, come on, you WON. We received that notification from Marco that everything was progressing to plan back at Baka's estate, and look, given the odds of what we took on today, that's one hell of a fight that we took to them. How could we ever have thought he would bring what had to be about half his army to just take on the 'warrior princess' of Colombia? And not for nothing, other than some ugly bumps and bruises that you incurred during the most hellacious fighting I have ever seen, you are still in pretty good shape. Which is a very good thing because I am still counting on you to get us the hell out of here."

The whole time Chris is prodding and smiling at his beloved Ana. Ana turns to Chris. "How do you do that? In the worst of times, keep me sane? I love you so much, and yet I have risked your life without any hesitation."

Chris responds, "Like I've told you before, without you, there is no life for me. We are joined at the hip."

Interrupting their dialogue, Baka shouts out, "Whoever is held up in the remains of that Church, you need to surrender or come out shooting. We have you heavily outnumbered and, by the limited firepower we've heard, outgunned. So, what will it be? You have fifteen minutes to decide."

Chris says to Ana, "You know, one of my favorite movies is Butch Cassidy and Sundance."

Ana responds, "Yeah, and what? You're thinking of running out there, guns blazing, and you can barely run?"

Chris responds, "Well, I was thinking we surprise them with our bold move, and you focus on everyone you can see on the left, and I will take everyone on the right. It's better than letting that son of a bitch have his way with us because you know what he has in store for us should we surrender. This would be a lot quicker and force his hand to take us out right there."

"To be honest, Chris, that was my initial thought as well. I just didn't want to accept the fact that was our best and only option at this point."

While Chris and Ana start to gather whatever ammunition they have while reloading their weapons and securing any random grenades, Ana now starts to help Chris up, and with that, the snake (Baka) enters with his soldiers.

"Well, well. Look at this lovely picture. You should have known you couldn't trust me to give you those fifteen minutes. See men? Good things come to those who wait. Look whose prayers are answered. Seems like 'El Diablo' still has sovereignty here in Colombia."

Chris, exhibiting their defiant spirit, speaks, "Baka, do you really think what? You and your six men have any chance against Ana and me?"

Baka almost chuckles. "I can see why Ana would fall for someone like you, very ballsy, but you and I have a little score to settle yet, even though I can see you already have picked up a few wounds. So why don't I help by ending your needless suffering? Baka asks one of his soldiers to remove his bayonet and hand it over to Baka.

Ana desperately tries to intervene. "Baka, why are you fussing with Chris? It is me you have always wanted. There's nothing Chris can do to harm you anymore. Just let him be. He is badly injured as it is."

"See?" addressing his men, "this is what I hoped for. Whatever additional pain I inflict on this Chris person will bring even more pain to Ana. Talk about a win-win situation for me," Baka says, now chuckling.

Ana tries to quickly go after Baka but is subdued and held back by his soldiers. Ana still pleads for Chris's safety, but to no avail.

Baka now instructs two of his men to hold Chris as he slowly approaches. "I think your time has finally come to an end, Chris. Let me just plant this thought in your head to ease the new pain you will soon feel. It will be nothing compared to what the love of your life is going to endure."

With that said, Baka plunges the bayonet into Chris's stomach, and Chris falls to his knees in agony. Ana pulls away from her captors, and Baka allows her to try and comfort Chris. Trying to hold it together, Chris whispers to Ana, "I love you more than ever," struggling more than ever to continue speaking, breathing heavily, "and it really would be great if you find a way out of all of this and come back to me. I have only one request. Promise me you will call out to Arielle before that bastard has his way with you. She is your only hope now."

Ana, sobbing, says, "I promise, Chris, and now you promise me to hang on and not die on me. I also promise I will be back for you and get you help."

Chris whispers one more request, "One more thing, when you kill that mother fucker, will you chop his fucking head off for me?"

Ana is pulled away by her captors. Baka smiles with great satisfaction. "I don't know about the rest of you, but I am loving this." He orders one of his soldiers to take a picture of the suffering couple. "I may have that picture framed on one of my walls. Well, that's enough mercy on my part. Grab Ana as we have to take a little trip to one of my favorite playgrounds, the fire pit." They bind the still sobbing Ana's hands behind her back.

Baka instructs his men to put Ana in the second of the two awaiting jeeps. Baka turns to Chris, who's in misery. "Maybe next time you will pick a better mate. Oh, my mistake. There will be no next time for you."

Laughing at his own comment, Baka hops into the jeep with Ana in the back and two of his soldiers, one driving and the other seated in the back next to Ana. The other four soldiers pile into the lead jeep, and they take off to Baka's fire pit. As Chris watches the two jeeps pull away, fate intervenes and offers one small glimmer of hope. The first jeep, as it nears an uneven dirt road, suddenly explodes as it finds one of the few remaining landmines, killing all four occupants. Baka and Ana, with his two remaining soldiers, look aghast in the second jeep and can only try and shelter themselves from the scattering and falling debris. Baka, furious as ever, just explodes into a tirade against Ana in mixed Colombian and English with every conceivable profanity and how this is only going to make her punishment even more excruciating.

Chris, now half sitting and lying against some random concrete debris, sees a small truck pull up with a small group of nuns that may have previously worked at this mission site years ago to provide whatever care they can for the wounded.

Talking quietly to himself as he feels his life ebbing away, "Hey, Arielle, wherever you are, and you better be near for Ana's sake because this grand plan of yours sure has turned to shit. I, for one, am not too pleased with how this all turned out. What about a happy ever after ending? You know, a white picket fence and kids playing ball with Mom and Dad in the yard. Or how about me just hanging out at my beach house? Possibly just drinking myself to death seems to be a much better way to go than what I am looking at now. You really hooked me with all that 'is this how you really want to spend the rest of your whole life?' Yeah, I know, on the other hand you did lead me to Marisa, I mean Ana, and for a brief time, yes, my life with her was the greatest thing that ever happened to me, and so now I am paying the price, but you could have stopped at just a few minor wounds. My life is slipping away lying here, not exactly what I had in mind. I know what you would say. Now is the time I should be praying. Yeah, pray, Chris . . . pray."

His soft, weak voice trails off, and with that, Chris's vision blurs, and he can literally feel his body starting to shut down between the loss of blood and the sheer pain of his wounds; it is all just too overwhelming. As his eyes close, he suddenly feels a cool and comforting cloth wipe his forehead and face.

Struggling to gain consciousness and vision clarity, Chris is shocked at who is now by his side. Kneeling in a luminous bluish-gray robe is a remarkably familiar face, Theresa! Straining to get his voice and mind in sync, "Theresa, is this really you? Here... now? What is happening? You died in that car crash... wait, I get it, you are here to escort me through those heavenly gates."

Managing a slim smile, Theresa responds, "And why would you think you would be so deserving of such a fate, Chris?"

"My God, it really is you. What are you doing here?"

"Well, I think that is obvious. I am here to help you get back on your feet, as I understand they have some big plans for you."

"Again, with these frigging plans, you have got to be kidding me. Do you see that I am dying here? I don't even know how I am still able to talk with you."

Theresa responds, "Boy, you do take a girl for granted. Don't you remember my last words to you? 'I will always be by your side, and here I am.' You see, Chris, you and I were always meant to be together, just not in the way either of us could ever have imagined."

Chris responds with disbelief, "Wait, are you saying that... you are my... Angel? You're my Guardian Angel?"

"If that is what you want to call it, we can go with that. I have lots of assignments in my new role, but you are one of my priorities, so yes, we can go with the whole Guardian Angel thing, and besides, would there ever be anyone better than me? It really is miraculous how they figure all this life stuff out. It just took a lot of prodding on their part to get you to go along with the bigger picture, you are one stubborn believer, but as you can see after all your conversations with Arielle and that little mixture of Marisa and me and the evolution of Ana, this was always the plan.

"As for me, my untimely death was the best thing that ever happened to me. I have seen and experienced a new life that is beyond any human comprehension. I couldn't be happier and at peace, and as a bonus, I get to babysit you occasionally."

Chris is now starting to fade swiftly, but with a huge grin on his face.

Theresa says, "Hey, big guy, before you go anywhere, you and I need to do some heavy praying. This is serious now." With that and one wave of her hand, her robe enshrouds the both of them.

Chris whispers, "I hope that includes a new body because this one is pretty used up right now and maybe you could sneak in a little superpower or something."

Shaking her head at his silliness, Theresa tells him when he awakens from his imminent slumber he will feel like a new man, and with that they pray as Chris soon slips into a comatose-like sleep.

Baka and Ana finally arrive at their destination along with his two soldiers. Ana soon sees why Baka referred to this location as his fire pit playground. There is a rather tall steel pole which serves as a post in which Baka places his victims and surrounds them with kindling. The surrounding area is littered with bones and even a few skulls from former poor unfortunate souls. This is his own personal hell for his victims. The one soldier pulls Ana from the jeep, and they throw her to the ground as there is not much she can do with her hands tightly bound behind her back. The one soldier suggests to Baka that first he let the two soldiers have some fun before Baka begins his torture routine.

The one soldier says, "This is a fine-looking woman and who wouldn't want some of that."

Baka replies, "Sure, just don't get careless. She is a tiger."

With that, the one soldier approaches her with his rather large knife drawn and rips open her army blouse. "Now that's what I am talking about," referring to her ample sized breasts.

Ana is not going to make this easy for anyone and so she stands now as he approaches her again, and this time, like a flash, kicks him right in his crotch. He falls on his knees in great pain cursing Ana and with that the other soldier slams the back of Ana's head with his pistol, driving her to the ground.

Baka just sits on the side of his jeep, shaking his head and observing the whole scene as he is enjoying this little show. Lying on the ground and slowly rising to her knees, Ana starts in a barely audible whisper to herself, "Arielle, wherever or whoever you are I need you. If Chris believes in you, so do I. Please, please, help me."

As the one injured soldier staggers to his feet, the other one orders her to remove her blouse and pants. However, something high in the sky and off in the distance catches Baka's eye. It appears to be a rather unusually large bird heading in their direction. Now Colombia is known for their large Andean Condors, which are basically vultures, so he is not all that surprised to see one flying in their direction. What does start to raise his interest level is the speed at which this bird seems to be approaching their location although at quite a height.

Baka now calls over to his soldiers before they continue with their antics with Ana. "Check out the size of the Condor that is heading this way." Pointing in the direction of the approaching bird.

As the bird is well within everyone's eyesight now, Baka speaks up again. "I have never seen a Condor fly that fast and in such a direct line and look at the size of that bird, and its enormous wing-span."

The one soldier, laughing says, "Well he may be getting ready for dinner, but tell him it is too early yet; we haven't even started the fire."

"Wait a minute," says Baka as the massive bird is maybe a little more than a hundred yards away and is starting a descent more like a dive directly to their location. "What the hell, get your guns ready, that's no Condor, it's more like a giant eagle of some kind and it's started a dive like it's found its prey."

Before they can even get any shots off, the majestic eagle swoops down and without slowing down grabs the two soldiers, one in each talon, and heads right back up into the sky.

Stunned, Baka is now firing wildly at the immense bird, which doesn't skip a beat and continues skyward flying like a missile with a mission. Suddenly and without any reason, the massive eagle just drops the two soldiers from a great height, and they plunge to their deaths. Given what they have just witnessed both Baka and Ana are temporarily speechless.

"What the fuck was that?" Baka asked Ana as if she has any answers.

Pointing his automatic rifle at Ana, Baka says, in a more accusatory tone, "I don't know how or why, but somehow you are responsible for all of this. First the fucking jeep blows up with some of my best troops and now this, leaving just you and me, which is now even more unfortunate for you because now I am going to inflict the slowest, most horrible pain I ever have on one person. Then, after watching you burn to death; I am going to physically rip your fucking head from your body."

Baka continues his tirade and instructs Ana to move over to the pole and keep removing her clothes, as he wants her completely naked on the stake. Ana starts to slowly remove her clothes not saying a word because she just caught a glimpse, without giving anything away, of the returning majestic eagle, but Baka has his back turned to the incoming bird. Again, the colossal eagle, flying at incredible speeds, swoops down and slams Baka to the ground with such force that almost knocks him unconscious and sends his weapon flying. At the same time, the giant bird drops a metallic object from its talons behind Ana. Seizing on her opportunity, Ana quickly adjusts her clothing and searches for that metallic object that the eagle dropped in her direction. Ana picks it up and to her amazement it is her father's sword, one of his prized possessions that he had made as a family heirloom. The only person he ever let use of it was Ana when it became apparent that she possessed these incredible youthful skills working with her trainers. The majestic eagle circling their location now takes off skyward and eventually over the horizon.

Baka stumbles to his feet and looks over at Ana standing before him with her sword at her side. Baka weekly attempts to grab his handgun from his side and Ana speaks. "Don't even think about it. As a matter of fact, very slowly unbuckle and drop that gun belt or feel my blade."

Baka begrudgingly complies. "I knew it. I don't know or understand how an enormous eagle comes to your aid, but clearly that is what happened. But this is far from over."

"Baka, let me refresh your sodden memory? What is the Moreno family crest?"

Baka takes a moment. "The flaming eagles. Are you kidding me? Have you become some kind of sorceress or something? That was no bird, that was a beast."

"Honestly, I am as amazed as you are and what and why are way beyond me. But unlike you, I am going to give you the opportunity of a lifetime. I know you also have a special sword that you like to use for all your joyful beheadings. I hope you brought it with you."

"Yes, it is in the back of my jeep. Let me get it."

"You stay right there." Ana now picks up Baka's automatic pistol in her other hand and searches the back of his jeep. Finding his blood-stained sword, she throws it over to him. "Pick it up,

Baka, and I will give you the chance you have dreamed of . . . killing me with your own hands. Only one of us is walking away from here today, and the other one is going to suffer a very painful death."

Baka happily picks up his sword, telling Ana, "Do you have any idea how many men I have killed in battle with this sword aside from all the beheadings? I will do you the honor of being my last kill and beheading."

"For me, Baka, I have waited a long, painful time to avenge my father's and brother's deaths, and for what you did to my beloved Chris. I am fueled with an anger that you will soon feel at the edge of my blade. Let the battle begin." And with that, they square off.

As the sun starts to set, their fierce battle begins. Sizing each other up, they both attack with strong and powerful blows as their blades clash violently. It soon becomes apparent to Baka that he is no match for the younger, quicker, and more agile Ana and that she is well-schooled in the use of this lethal weapon. Baka realizes he must try something unorthodox or from his book of dirty tricks. As he decides to make an unexpected quick move to slash her leg, hoping to disable her, Ana counters at the opening and plunges her sword deep into Baka's chest.

Stunned in disbelief with a trickle of blood dripping from his mouth and just staring at Ana, he falls to his knees. "That is for my father, and now this is for my brother." She thrust the sword deeper while twisting the blade. Baka crumbles to the ground; the Colombian devil is dead. Still filled with anger and hate, Ana withdraws her blade. She props Baka up against a large rock and, gathering as much strength as she has left in her weary war-torn body, "And this is for Chris." With one ferocious swing of her blade, she severs Baka's head and sends it rolling to the ground. She then extends her sword to the heavens and shouts, "for my family, for Chris, for Colombia, and my Savior!"

Exhausted, Ana thrusts her sword into the ground at her feet and falls to her knees. Feeling an incredible range of emotions, she starts weeping silently, trying to clear her mind of all that has transpired on this day. All the coordinated planning, a burning vengeance placated, a feeling of satisfaction yet, an air of despair overwhelms her at the same time ----just too many mixed emotions. Her primary goal achieved; her father and brother have been avenged, but at what cost, weeping more heavily, thinking about all those courageous soldiers that fought so hard and gave of themselves to her cause, and Chris, the love of her life. In the midst of her sorrows, she tries to console herself, knowing now that her countrymen and women can live their lives free from tyranny and terror and their daughters can dream again of having their lives filled with love and bliss as there will be no more kidnappings, etc.

Yet, now more than ever, for Ana personally, there is a new feeling of dread and gloom. What does her future hold with no Chris by her side? His easy manner of making her feel comfort and joy at the most perilous times, to say nothing of the great love they shared and bright future.

Ana starts speaking a soft soliloquy to herself, "I could have never accomplished this unbelievable victory without him. He is the love of my life, and while my heart is filled with gratification, it grows heavy at the thought of having no future without him. I can only thank my Lord and Savior for the wondrous times we spent together, and for the bravery of those incredible soldiers that gave their lives for my countrymen. More than anything, I should be thankful for the overwhelming victory we all have achieved. Oh, and please thank Arielle for hearing my plea. This final victory over evil could never have been accomplished without her remarkable assistance. That massive eagle was amazing and still hard to believe."

"YOU'RE WELCOME."

Startled from her soliloquy, Ana looks up, and over to her left, about fifteen feet away, is an astonishing luminous angelic figure with dazzling blue eyes standing in a pristine white robe and a broad smile on her face, Arielle.

Stammering to find the words. "You're Arielle?"

"Yes, Ana, as you requested." Ana responds with amazement as to what she is witnessing, "And it was you who sent that beautiful, majestic eagle that saved my life?"

"Yes, again, you were in a rather desperate situation, and something had to be done quickly."

"Who are you? And how does Chris know about you? Are you a spiritual messenger or an Angel?"

"I guess after all you have been through, it is time for some revelations. Your faith has always been strong, so believe it or not, I am your 'Angelic Guide,' or 'Guardian' if you prefer, but I was sent to you for an incredibly special purpose, which is why we are both here in this time and place celebrating a victory of good over evil. A great mission has been accomplished today by two extraordinary special people with a little help from their new friends from above."

"Oh my God, I can't believe any of this. I don't understand what is happening. Baka is finally dead, massive eagles, the enormous battle back at Baka's estate, all those good men that died today, Chris gone from my life, and now your unreal and mind-boggling presence. This is all too much for me to take in and digest. My mind is swirling. Are you really here talking to me, or am I becoming delusional?"

"Take heart, Ana. Let's focus on what you have achieved with your comrade's heroic efforts. You have eliminated years of misery, fear, corruption and evil, to say nothing of the possibility of saving hundreds of lives for generations to come. You have lifted the veil of tyranny, malevolence, and suppression that the villagers and farmers had to deal with in their everyday lives. You have given them hope and dreams of a better life. Yes, a great many people have sacrificed much, but when you look at what you and your soldiers in arms have returned to them, it really is a great victory for the people of Colombia and for good over evil for years to come, just think of the sociological ripple effect . . . like throwing a rock in a lake, it is all good."

Ana is calmer and more pensive now. "I can see why I lucked out having such a great spiritual advisor as you, Arielle. I hope you will always be there for me in my time of need or just point me in the right direction. How does someone possibly thank you or honor you for all that you have done for me?"

"Ana, it is I who should be thanking you and Chris. It is short of miraculous what the two of you have accomplished and who knows, there may be some new and exciting challenges for the two of you down the road."

Ana stares at Arielle in disbelief. "Did I just hear you correctly? Are you referring to Chris? Because there is no way he can still be alive. I know what Baka did to him before I left his mortally wounded body."

Arielle responds all knowingly, "You keep saying Chris is gone, and for the first time, you doubt your faith in all that has happened today. As I said, this is a truly miraculous day, and maybe they extend even further down your road."

"Are you saying Chris is still alive? There's no way. I just can't believe that."

Arielle smiles. "But you can believe in giant eagles coming out of nowhere and delivering your father's sword to you?"

"Oh, my God, I must go immediately, but how . . . how do I ever thank you?"

Arielle responds, "Just keep living the life you have so far and never change. Keep believing and please think of me and send me your prayers as I will always be at your side, not always visible like this, but I am here for you."

Ana is bursting with tears of joy. "I love you, Arielle."

"And I love you, Ana. Please do one little favor for me. Tell Chris I really enjoyed our little chats and that his decision to change the direction of his life has made an extraordinary difference in potentially thousands of lives."

Jumping into the jeep, Ana takes off brimming with anxiety about the prospect of seeing Chris alive, regardless of how badly he may still be injured.

Back at the mission, Chris is awakened again by a cool, comforting cloth wiping his forehead and face. As his vision clears, stammering at the stranger caring for him, he says, "You're not Theresa. I'm sorry, sister." It is one of the other nuns caring for him. "Where's the nun in the blue-gray robe? Her name is Theresa."

The nun replies, "I'm sorry, but we don't wear robes, and we don't have any sisters that go by the name of Theresa. You might have suffered a bad concussion and maybe dreamt it; the mind can play funny tricks on us when we experience this type of injury."

With that, Chris soon realizes that all those horrific pains are gone. He reaches down to his stomach, and there is no blade. What's more, there is no hint of any stomach injury or bullet wound in his shoulder. "Excuse me, sister, and thank you so much for your assistance, but I need to check on a few things. Thank you again."

"You are quite welcome, my son. Feel better and be safe out there."

Chris is trying to get his bearings and reaches over to his injured shoulder, which is pain-free and good as new. He bends his injured leg looking for where he had been hit with the shrapnel, and there is just one minor wound that remains on his leg.

Looking up and talking to no one in particular, "Really? You heal all my wounds and take away all my pain and not for nothing save my life, and you leave this one stinking little wound? You still haven't lost that sarcastic humor of yours." Chris pauses. "Hey, wherever you are, Theresa, thank you. Thank you for saving my life, and yeah, just the thought you will always be by my side spiritually is very comforting. I love you, Theresa."

Chris rises to his feet, no idea how long he has been out, and starts to run around to find a vehicle he can use to head out and find Ana. While he is gimping around trying to find someone or a car he can use, he sees a very dusty jeep pull up, but the headlights blind him as dusk has fallen. With that, out jumps a very familiar figure sprinting to his location. Ana abruptly stops her sprint within feet of Chris, trying to fight through her emotions to grab him but also in amazement that there he is, standing, seemingly free of any wounds and staring right back at her. Tears stream down Ana's face.

They embrace, and Ana almost knocks him over as she starts shouting, "You're alive and standing." They hug each other tightly as ever and kiss one another deeply, and then suddenly stop. Ana steps back. "How is this possible? I know what I saw and how badly injured you were when I left. You were dying."

"Man, you really know how to make a guy feel good about himself," Chris responds sarcastically.

"Come on, Chris, you know what I mean. How did this happen?"

"Tell you what, first, you tell me how you got away from Baka and is he alive or dead, by the way?"

"No, he is very, very dead, and yes, he is definitely missing his head. Baka is gone forever."

Chris responds, "Unbelievable. Remind me never to make you angry."

Ana replies, smiling, "Oh, and by the way, I did meet your good friend, Arielle, and this is one truly miraculous day."

Chris responds, "Wow, so we both have a lot to catch up on, but you know what; we need to stick to the original plan and get the hell out of here because this place is going to be flooded with all kinds of Colombian and U.S. authorities.

"We need to find a phone and contact our friends to see if that one chopper is still waiting for us in our planned designated location so we can get back to Gorgona."

They hop into Ana's jeep and take off to the remains of Baka's estate. They eventually meet up with Cousin Marco and tell him the good news about Baka's fate and where to find his remains for those that want any proof. As word spreads of Baka's demise, there are renewed celebrations and cheering as Marco sets Ana and Chris up in a jeep they can take to the still-waiting Chopper.

As they ride through the sometimes very densely wooded roads to their secret destination, sharing their incredible experiences, Chris, as usual, brings Ana back to earth as she is filled with unbridled joy and pride at the way everything has turned out.

As they are getting ready to board the chopper, Chris says to Ana, "So if what you are telling me about Baka is really true, then it was 'Big Bird' that really saved you."

Ana, in her loving but usual flippant tone when he pokes fun at her, replies, "You're still such an ass, but an ass that I will treasure forever."

The chopper rises swiftly into the night sky. Ana and Chris embrace with an abundance of thoughts, emotions, and amazement over what they both have experienced and what new adventures may lie ahead.

About the Author

Mr. Borak is currently retired and previously worked in Sr. Management for the Project Management Office (PMO) at the state of New Jersey, Department of Human Services. Over the years prior to his taking the position with the State, he was an independent Management Consultant for mostly Fortune 100 Companies (AT&T Corporate, Bloomberg Financial, NBC, Pfizer, Merck, Prudential Insurance, Chase Morgan, etc.)

Subsequently, he has a wealth of experiences to draw from life, family and business. This led to writing articles, short stories, etc. that he would periodically submit to local newspapers or various magazines. William also composed a business case chapter in a technology related text book (Data Management, Barbara von Halle and David Kull, Editors, published by Auerbach Publications, Boston and New York).

William is a life long NJ resident, currently living in Monmouth County and graduated from Rutgers University. Unfortunately, he was diagnosed with Parkinsons disease about 9 years ago however, despite those struggles and difficult days, he was able to fulfill a lifelong dream of having his first novel published.

A Note from Literary Titan about their awards:

Our *Literary Awards* are given to books and authors that have astounded and amazed us with unique writing styles, vivid worlds, complex characters, and original ideas. These books deserve extraordinary praise and we are proud to acknowledge the hard work, dedication, and writing skill of talented authors.

The *Gold Award* is bestowed on books that we found to be perfect in their delivery of original content, meticulous development of unique characters in an organic and striking setting, innovative plot that supports a fresh theme, and elegant prose that transforms words into beautifully written books.

Made in the USA
Middletown, DE
22 October 2023